BETRAYAL

Part 5

Affairs of the Heart Series ~ London

KEW TOWNSEND

Tremmelle Publishing

HOLLYWOOD, CALIFORNIA

© 2016 Tremmelle Publishing, United States
© 2015 Cover Design by Sparkle Graphics
© 2015 Cover Layout by Jesse Kimmel-Freeman
© 2015 Cover images by Podaboty; By-Studio
© 2014 Book Layout BookDesignTemplates.com

Sign up for NEWSLETTER at www.kewtownsend.com

BETRAYAL/KEW Townsend
ISBN 978-06925007-0-5

Affairs of the Heart Series
London

HEART (Part 1)
TEMPTATION (Part 2)
PROMISES (Part 3)
DEVOTED (Part 4)

Affairs of the Heart Series
Hollywood

BLOOD (Part 1)
SURRENDER (Part 2)
LIASION (Part 3)
DECEPTION (Part 4)

Sign up for NEWSLETTER

kewtownsend.com

CONTENTS

Chapter One

OVER THE EDGE

August 1989

London, England

Day 5

The sleek white limo cut through the wet, cobblestone streets of London. Pedal to the metal, it passed the Dickens' street lamps well beyond the speed limit. The occupants raced against the clock as the limo sped pass timeworn buildings.

Holly Hill closed her eyes counting her breaths. She sat on the edge of her seat between Luka Hunter and Kaine Walker waiting for the explosion. Two bodyguards sat far away in the front seat. Ian Montgomery and Solange Beauvais followed behind in a private car.

Yes — Luka was back!

Worse than expected.

Her heart pounded because his body touched hers. She grabbed a short breath and leaned into Kaine.

She wanted Luka to go away — to vanish.

Luka sat close, very, very close to her. His firm body leaned closer. Too, close. How was it that he molded so quickly to her, his side fit perfectly against her body and she enjoyed the burn? His fresh scent cut a path through Kaine's personable blend and wrapped around her senses, jogging her memories of Luka and his wonderful, sexy fragrance.

Luka's damp blond hair reminded her he had been naked when he washed his hair. It hung long with rebellious strands draped over her shoulder, weaving itself into hers, prompting recollections of better times with her powerful angel.

Luka, handsome and elegantly dressed, sat regally posed a handmade two-button Asset suit. It was a soft, creamy-beige, cashmere wool blend. Underneath, a pale blue and white, thin striped silk shirt with a banded collar, to match those fucking beautiful eyes she felt staring a hole through her. His long, lean legs, were cloaked with the expensive trouser material, cuffed at the bottom and were rubbing against her leg. His shoes suede, with a sleek capped toe.

Another fucking elegant man.

She fought the renegade thoughts running rampant in her mind. She recalled his icy blue eyes in the elevator asking why.

Why?

Kaine was why.

Why didn't Luka understand?

The silence proved to be deafening.

The limo hit a bump jolting Holly. She glanced up to Luka, who behaved unusually somber. She settled back into the quiet and solitude of the car, her mind racing on the cocaine she'd inhaled. What caused everyone's anxiety?

An evil omen crept inside Holly.

She shifted her eyes quickly to glance at Kaine. Though his eyes were alert; his face appeared sallow, drawn, and easy to presume he hadn't slept much the last two days. He must be burnt out and running on pure cocaine.

She realized she was like him and not slept. She couldn't pinpoint the last time either of them had eaten anything resembling a meal.

What happened to her?

A brittle chill settled inside, pushing her to snuggle up against Kaine and wrap her arms around the trunk of his body to soak in his warmth.

He closed his arms around her, squeezed her tight as if reading her mind, and consoled.

"Don't worry sweetheart," he reassured in her ear. "Everything's going to be perfect after tonight. Soon I will have everything I have ever wanted or dared to dream."

Holly looked out the window watching the storm blown shadows. The rain slapped the sides of the limousine with a hard sheet of water.

Another rain drenched night.

She hated them.

Occasional lights in the English countryside danced in the rain for her. She hoped Kaine was right because she couldn't shake the dreadful fear, taking root inside her. All of Solange's warnings plagued her and realizing this was a major headline event, there was so much to remember. The undercover reporters, the A-guest list, her new status as the mystery woman, caused her head to swim. Plus the thought of having to sit without Kaine for the next few hours, while they played a modified setlist from Wembley, did not settle well. She was thankful she had media savvy Solange, instead of Luka, and not have to battle this siege alone.

Holly nestled even closer to bask in Kaine's heat and comfort. She drank in his familiar cologne scent as the car jerked and changed gears, then slowed down while the adrenaline flowed faster in her veins. Glancing beyond the dark partitioning, she saw a steady row of serpentine red taillights.

The car slowed.

Luka pulled a vial from his pocket. "This is the best I was able to find."

Holly and Kaine took turns until the bottle was empty. She was no judge of quality, but this cocaine seemed more powerful. Or, was it the quantity she'd ingested?

She sat back leaning on Kaine's shoulder, hoping her head would not blow apart.

Luka yelled to the driver.

"Pass the fuckers! We're bloody late!"

Chapter Two

IN THE AIR TONIGHT

The limousine pulled off to the side of the road. It jerked as it settled into the rutted shoulder of the pathway. For twenty nerve-wracking minutes, it jolted its internationally famous guests until the Unholy Trinity arrived in front of the black, malevolent gates.

An uninvited panic swept over Holly as she stared at the ugly, monstrous, twenty-foot wall that protected the elite of rock 'n' roll. The limo stopped at the wrought-iron gate, then inched closer to the three-story, Gothic monument, built as a reminder of a long forgotten time. She barely made out the main facade of the building obstructed by the blinding rain. Tall demons aligned the carved alcoves in the shape of hideous bats with wings stood guard on each side of the imposing crenelated roof.

She whispered calming thoughts to herself as she passed through the gates of Hell.

Dread twisted around Holly's stomach. Where were the joyous feelings, celebrating *Hurrikaine's* triumphant arrival?

The only hints of joy were the bars of lights pouring out of the ground floor, stained-glass windows scattering a kaleidoscope of rainbow colors. The car crept up a narrow, obscure driveway far from the guest entrance at the west wing.

A small group of people waited like elves, with open umbrellas to assist the celebrated guests out of their car. They quickly escorted them past an arched alcove and then inside the hideous brick building. They ushered Holly and her famous lover down a long, darkened corridor until they came to a well-lit area.

Towering beside her were wine-tinted, velvet curtains. Behind them stretched a timeworn, well-tended stage and the band's equipment. Michael Evans sat behind his drums nervously spinning his drumsticks between his fingers. Chris Taylor held his bass guitar perched on his leg lightly thumbing his top E-string. Nicky Jamison fiddled about tuning his Telecaster guitar. Holly came to the same conclusion as always. *Hurrikaine* was one hell of a good-looking band.

Nicky's face shined when he looked up with his soft, green eyes, full of allegiance, reflected his pleasure to find their leader arrived and announced, "Kaine's here, now we need Ian. Let's get this fucking show over with and start breathing again," he exclaimed with a great big warm smile.

Holly wasn't sure Kaine heard Nicky announce his arrival because he abruptly pulled her away from everyone. He backed into a dark alcove where he leaned close, oh so close, his hot breath blowing near her diamond. His hot, moist lips pressed against the flesh of her earlobe, sending light electric flashes, forcing her breath to accelerate. Her heart pounded a steady beat, following Michael's drum. He continued a trail of moist, hot kisses across her cheek to her lips.

When he arrived, she hungered for him.

Kaine pulled her back a bit more out of the circle of attention.

She surrendered, as his hands went up inside her full-length leather coat, up around her naked spine and his cool fingertips excited her, like flashing lightning, skimming along the top of the water. His heart was pounding onto her breasts while his lips sucked. She returned his blazing, cocaine, driven passion, with equal zeal, positive that if he did not let go of her soon, he would simply crawl inside her skin. His kisses were deep and compelling. An alarming sense of intoxication swamped her as the cocaine wrapped his love around her heart and promised to explode with pure ecstasy.

When the sounds of the world demanded they give it their attention, she was lost in the dream state. Then Kaine, relaxed, releasing her from his sacred embrace.

"No, don't," she said softly into his mouth.

Holly didn't want to be away from Kaine. Her fingers quickly dropped from his long, silky hair, loosely secured behind his head with a black velvet cord. A long lock fell tickling her face and hung alone next to his jaw line. She blindly hung it over his ear. Her eyelids hung heavy with love. She gazed at him with half-lidded eyes, and she watched her thumb pull on his lower lip. She closed her glazed eyes, knowing she behaved unreasonably, but that realization did not seem to stop her.

Kaine took her hands from his face.

She smiled as the warmth of his lips kissed each fingertip, weaning her from him. She refused to open her eyes to acknowledge he would leave her soon.

"Holly, sweetheart," Kaine called more insistent, but quietly, to bring her to attention. He shook her a bit. "My Lady, don't worry. I love you. After tonight, everything will be perfect. Hold on for a few more hours because after midnight, we can start our life together," Kaine reminded before he kissed her quickly.

Against her will, she opened her eyes, and they locked onto his filled with so much concern for her. His soft, alluring blue colored eyes invited her deeper and deeper into his heart and he whispered, "Tonight I sing only for you," his voice, smooth, smoldering, that she heard with her heart.

The cold rushed in all about her, a quaking cold as the familiar hand slid around her waist, pulling her away from Kaine.

"Come on! We're late!" Luka commanded his voice harsh, irritated, as his hand firmly grasped a hold of Holly's waist and jerked her from Kaine's embrace.

"It is showtime," Luka stated. Then, he enthusiastically handed Holly over to Solange with instructions.

"Take her with you. Kaine needs to prepare."

Holly's heart sank deeper into melancholy with each step she took away from Kaine. She looked back over her shoulder. Kaine handed his long, black, velvet overcoat to Ian, dressed in a single-breasted, black-pinstripe Asset suit, so familiar, and expected. Under the coat, he wore a purple, long-sleeved silk shirt with a matching black waistcoat, another elegant man.

She glanced back to Kaine and looked sadly into his eyes. None of them looked like rock stars, perhaps more like a misplaced group of wealthy executives seeking an evening's fun. It was evident that they wore their own version of a rock 'n' roll image, not letting the image of rock 'n' roll wear them.

"It is okay, sweetheart." Kaine consoled loudly, but easily to Holly, clearly upset by her clinging behavior.

It may be okay for him to let her go, but it suddenly wasn't okay for her to let him go. She didn't understand her own behavior. She surmised it must be the spooky manor, casting an evil spell over her. Its atmosphere created a dark sense of doom. And it clung heavily to her, causing her to drag her feet. She looked back one last time to admire her magnificent Kaine. He stood tall and elegant in his charcoal Asset suit.

At that moment, with the power of a baseball bat hitting her in the back of her head, she realized, the eye of the *Hurrikaine* was her man.

Solange took Holly to an out of the way area to catch her breath. Solange looked beautiful. She admired the handy work of the talented lady in the hotel salon. She'd swept her copper-colored hair up into a maze of spiral curls. She dressed in a tailored, dark-green velvet, strapless Asset gown, with a heart-shaped bodice, and bore a slit high up the side, revealing her fabulous lithe thigh. The faux fur-lined, beaded jacket seemed to be enough to keep Solange warm. She'd left her leather coat with Kaine, and wearing a thinner fabric, shook uncontrollably. It was very, very cold without Kaine.

Solange held Holly's hand and led her to the entrance of the manor where they joined Luka. He waited, leaning on the wall with his arms crossed over his chest. Luka grumbled under his breath as Holly followed him up to a well-dressed woman managing the guest list.

"Luka Hunter escorting Miss Holly Hill and Miss Solange

Beauvais," he announced. Then instantly they were escorted to the next door. Luka gave another well-dressed woman their names and again escorted like royalty into a mammoth, three-story, fifteenth-century ballroom. In its time, Holly was positive kings and queens must have graced the highly polished floor.

Holly quickly glanced about the regal banquet room, noting there must be a hundred tables eloquently set with exquisite tableware. She'd never experienced anything like the grandeur of the charming room. She became Cinderella, and it left her exhilarated but overwhelmed. The pungent air scented with fine cuisine; familiar scents like seafood and roasted fowl.

She noticed at the far end of the massive room, tiny, wine-colored curtains that hung to conceal the stage. As her eyes adjusted to the dim lighting, she saw to her surprise every eye looking at her. She lowered her chin as if bowing her head naturally, like a queen addressing her court.

Easily, she slipped her hand into Luka's as natural as taking a breath. He wrapped his strong hand around hers, giving her a squeeze, passing the necessary strength to pull off her sudden royal status with this imposing crowd.

She remembered Solange's instructions and followed a quarter step behind Luka, proud to be entering the room on his arm. His paced was of one of grandeur. His head held high, tipping slightly to greet people, and it seemed he knew them all. She was thankful he did not stop to make introductions at any of the tables, which comfortably seated ten guests. But Solange did and stayed behind to greet her friends. Holly and Luka continued to skirt the tables, and she noticed the army of waiters clearing away the dessert dishes.

Luka stayed close to the wall and then crossed to the center of the ballroom in front of the giant wine-colored curtains. She looked around and understood her arrival made her conspicuous as if she'd had a spotlight following her. But that had been the glow of envy from the eyes of those that watched her.

Luka pulled out a chair next to another beautiful woman. Holly found it difficult to find a comfortable way to sit with every eye on her. Luka bent and placed his warm cheek next to hers, his hair cascaded to the side, giving them a moment's privacy from the gawking audience. The scent of his sweet breath brushed her senses as he encouraged her.

"You're doing fine Babe, as I expected you would."

It took a moment to realize he had also pressed his soft lips lovingly on her cheek, kissing her because he loved her too. She forced a smile.

"That's right," he responded smoothly. "Keep smiling. Show them how beautiful you are. Everyone's curious about the Heart of the *Hurrikaine.*"

Holly stiffened. He was directing her again, reminding her, and Luka repeated the title she now wore with dread.

Luka slipped into a seat, leaving the one next to her empty. Her eyes searched his asking why.

Luka did not answer. He looked away and greeted the other guests at the table and then waved a young man over and ordered him to bring a cafe latté.

A chill set in reminding her she was alone. She glanced at the huge tent sign placed in the center of the exquisitely set table that reads.

Exclusively Reserved
HURRIKAINE AND GUESTS

After a series of short breaths, Holly glanced around the table to see her dinner companions by the candlelight. They tried not to stare at her, but it was impossible. She recognized their surprise, they all saw the return of a ghost — Carrin, and their faces wore the look of pure astonishment. Would this ever end?

Holly noticed three fashionably dressed women. Holly assumed they were either wives or girlfriends of the band. The women smiled a visible sigh of relief when Solange joined the group sliding between Holly and Luka. Holly realized that Luka had left the seat between them vacant to place Solange next to her for support. He was always thinking so far ahead of her.

"We were getting worried. It's so late! You've missed dinner." One woman hurriedly offered.

"Sorry to worry you. I'm nervous and can't eat a thing," Solange admitted and smiled to put her friends at ease.

"The traffic's bloody awful. We crawled about forever. Then for the last ten miles, we followed Kaine's driver and rode on the shoulder of the road."

They all nervously laughed at this though the situation wasn't funny at all. Nothing was funny. Again, Holly sensed the pressure, noting the women gave the impression of being tightly wound as Kaine and Luka.

Holly listened to one say with a proper British accent.

"It's one thing to play for a hundred thousand strangers and quite another to play for legends and heroes of their profession for the first time. Nicky's so nervous, he tried to eat a snack and it was difficult for him to keep it down."

Everyone agreed, and each shared their loved one's failed

coping abilities, except Holly. Her lover had been busy lavishing her with flowers, gifts, and his dreams. She observed the small talk seemed to defuse their nervousness.

Solange suddenly apologized. "Where is my head? You've all heard about Kaine's girlfriend. Wee? I am proud to introduce her. Please, give her a warm welcome into our exclusive *Hurrikaine* sorority. Holly Hill, the woman all of London is talking about over a cuppa. Holly, this lovely lady is Emily, Nicky's wife, Lyssa, Michael's fiancée, and Laura, Chris's wife."

Great! All married, or in a committed relationship, she noted. There would be stability on the road with Kaine and companionship when he was doing whatever it was rock stars do.

Laura, who sat on the other side of Holly, said with a twist of a Southern accent announcing she was from the US of A.

"You're the Heart of the *Hurrikaine?* I'm so glad to meet you, Holly." A warm, friendly smile graced her beautiful face, surrounded by an avalanche of blond curls. She wore a strapless, black, velvet gown and her piercing topaz-colored eyes glinted, with a desire to become Holly's friend. "I saw Kaine pick you up last night and carry you out. Too romantic!" She remarked as she faked a swoon.

Everyone joined in with full, happy smiles and friendly laughter. It was heartwarming to see how tightly knit these women were, and Holly wished to become a full-fledged sorority sister soon.

A waiter arrived, immaculately dressed in a mock tuxedo with tails. He poured champagne into Holly's glass and before anyone had theirs filled and raised for a toast, Holly had drained hers and then awaited a refill.

Solange covered Holly's hand for the briefest moment.

"Careful Holly, this champagne is Cristal, the best, and will go straight to your head."

Holly motioned for the waiter to refill her glass. Her mouth was so d..r..y. Champagne was exactly what Holly wanted, and lots of it, too dull her drug charged senses. The cocaine blasted her much higher than she had grown used to causing her thoughts to become fuzzy. Unable to remember all the caution's Solange had advised, her heart pounded, and she needed to drown her strong feelings of foreboding and apprehension.

Holly sat quietly between Solange and Laura, watching Luka. She observed how he reached over the tableware for an appetizer. She wanted to be near him, to quell the frightening feelings brewing below the surface of her calm facade.

He slid his eyes to the side as if expecting to find her looking at him. He turned his face to hers. His cool blue, dreamy eyes locked onto hers.

Luka Hunter, so incredibly handsome by candlelight. She didn't find questions lingering in his eyes any longer. She didn't find remorse. His eyes sparkled with a renewed hope and then they narrowed, telling her it was a matter of time. He popped the snack cracker piled with a squiggly salmon-colored paste into his mouth. He suggestively allowed his tongue to linger, brushing it across his lips. Lips that said it had been too long since he had kissed her. The pull to him was strong. And she wanted to stop the unmistakable fiery attraction that threatened her future with Kaine.

He was coming for her.

Holly caught herself and quickly glanced around the table to find all eyes had been watching Luka's provocative performance. No one said a word. Instead, they threw their curious gazes politely on to something else as if they'd never witnessed the intimate exchange between Luka and Holly. The burn of embarrassment flooded Holly's body, especially when it settled on her cheeks, overwhelmed by the intense attraction she always held for Luka.

Would it ever die?

Laura leaned in close and stated so matter-of-factly. "Am I alone, or does everyone see the unusual change in Kaine? He acting differently, so charming."

"He's a pleasure to be around because he's found happiness." Emily pointed out.

"He's beautiful. Love looks spectacular on him. Keep doing whatever you're doing," Laura teased as if to set the record straight, irritate Luka for his garish behavior, and punish him.

Luka took the bait. "Not for long," he blasted bitterly.

Usually the gentleman, Holly interpreted Luka's retort as being betrayed. Betrayal. Such an ugly word. The idea sets off another round of guilt making her acknowledge her sorrow that it was her angel-eyed Luka that had been bushwhacked in the crossfire of her blazing love affair with the eye of the *Hurrikaine*.

The ladies brushed off Luka's spoiled sport comment, laughing light heartily. But Holly watched everyone, each acutely aware she was trapped between Luka and Kaine. And they unanimously voted for Kaine. She dropped her head, would it ever end?

Kaine's conversion stayed the topic of conversation, forcing Luka to turn away and strike up an exchange with someone at the next table. The only glitch in her fairy tale romance was still Luka, and this fleeting glimpse into Luka's jealous side, told Holly, Kaine was right. Luka would never accept her with Kaine. Never!

Holly's feelings of fear and disaster grew stronger. Her intuition told her to find Kaine. If only to touch him before it was too late. She needed to believe everything was all right.

Suddenly the roll of Michael's drums startled her. It was showtime.

There was no chance now.

"Take it easy Holly." Solange cautioned as she laid her warm hand on Holly's arm to comfort her. "Sit and smile for Kaine. This is his night, and he needs you to be proud of him. Pretend we're back at the studio and he's singing to you."

"That's what he said to me Solange, he'd be singing to me."

"Well, please remember what he said. He needs to be able to focus because everyone he loves admires, or respects are in this audience. Keep your chin up and smile. If you need to, hold on to my hand."

She dropped it nonchalantly below the table line placing earplugs in Holly's hand and then left it there.

Holly joined the others, ceremoniously to protect their ears.

The always-recognizable music icon, Sir William Larchmont, walked out to reserved applause. After moments of appropriate recognition, the crowd sat back. Sir William delivered a quick account of the history of *Hurrikaine* and the long road to Friar Manor, and then he announced.

"Without further delay…

H-U-R-R-I — — — K-A-I-N-E!"

Chapter Three

AFTER MIDNIGHT

Nicky's lightning charged opening guitar lick held everyone captive. The curtains slowly opened to tease the audience. A single purple spotlight flooded Kaine, standing tall, calm, and poised, center stage in front of his microphone.

Holly's heart leaped to her throat as her eyes rested on the only man in the world she not only loved but also wanted as her children's father. Kaine Walker, the man of the hour, looked magnificent. He stood a devastatingly gorgeous man, unbelievably sexy, wearing a crème silk shirt, and waistcoat unbuttoned to the fourth button, enticing her, wishing her hands to touch his muscular chest.

The cheering from the audience crowded the room, making it tricky to distinguish Kaine's smooth voice humming a melody. The band's long, lazy introduction broke into chart-topper, "One Love."

Holly's heart buzzed as Kaine tantalized and enticed his audience though he appeared to be subduing his usual oozing sexuality, to no avail as the aristocratic girls and women squealed with delight.

It was the onset of a wicked performance as Holly watched her wonderful Kaine, not twenty feet in front of her, pinning her with his intense blue eyes, crooning the words to "One Love." The pounding of Michael's drums and the rumbling beat of Chris's bass pulsated up and down her drug drenched body. The music vibrated inside her, teasing her, reminding her of Kaine and his powerful and passionate lovemaking. The blistering scream of Nicky's lead guitar tore through her twisting like a tornado and Ian's melodic keyboard pattern blistered her skin as the heat of her love ignited like a match in a barrel of kerosene.

Kaine hung draped over his microphone. He leaned the stand down, pointed straight at Holly, and sang. "I'll love y-o-u..., always."

Holly barely heard the crowd going berserk, over the glorious love filling, and spilling out of her heart. Her face blushed with a scorching hot love. Kaine was in love and he loved her enough to scream it to anyone who would listen. Kaine the ultimate showman, a born actor if she'd ever seen one, loved what he did, loved what he was, and now he loved her too. Yet he didn't prance about the stage like in the arena. He centered himself and demanded everyone's attention. He made love with his smooth, melodic voice, the voice of love long forgotten and then rekindled. The voice of hope.

Solange leaned over and whispered to Holly.

"Close your mouth and smile. People are watching you."

Holly obeyed and then slammed back another half glass of champagne as Solange continued.

"The shocked look on your face, must mean you didn't

realize what a brilliant performer he is? Look around, most women and more than a few men want to sleep with your Kaine. Realize this moment. Understand he is happy because of you. That should put Luka into perspective. Look at that man love you. Kaine is your only future."

Hypnotized and taken under Kaine's love-drenched spell, Holly nodded her head in agreement and took another long drink of her champagne. It was difficult to reconcile the man she had spent the past four days with as the same man that magically entranced this elite gathering of musicians. She took another sip, and another and another.

The only time Holly's eyes did not gaze into Kaine's was when he took a break between songs to wet his mouth. As the performance started to resemble an abbreviated setlist from Wembley, Holly glanced around to notice that the crowd enviously watched her as he sang to her. The pressure was building, and she took another sip.

Kaine sang straight into her heart. The cocaine had her spinning.

Between songs, she overheard comments the ladies at the table made, marveling at Kaine's extraordinary behavior.

"Kaine's never acted like this. It's as if he is trying to impress her! I had no idea Kaine was that sexy! He's never sung to anyone."

A voice reminded, "Kaine hasn't had anyone to sing for in so long, maybe forever."

Holly smiled, listening to Emily, Nicky's wife, confirm in her crisp British accent.

"He's fallen in love and I'm truly happy for him. It's what he's wanted, what I've wanted for him for so long."

Everyone is privy to our love affair. It's no longer a secret.

The stage went black.

A single spotlight rested on Kaine.

Uncharacteristic of his usual position as lead singer, Kaine picked up a Stratocaster guitar. He strapped it on and started to play a soulful lead that turned into a bluesy cover of Howlin' Wolf's "Little Red Rooster." The assembly of rockers stood up clapping like converts at a prayer meeting, as the soulful vibrato cries of John Roberts's Stratocaster rang out, echoing in the massive century's old hall. From the edge of the stage, a spotlight followed John as he strolled out blasting his legendary chops. One by one, the elite of the music world joined Kaine. They jammed and sang their hearts out and mesmerized the audience. With the last string plucked and cymbal struck, the powerhouse band took a bow and then walked off the stage, except *Hurrikaine.*

The room sat dumbfounded, stunned by the celestial jam. Then one after another, the members of the audience clapped, gaining momentum by the second, until the room roared with clapping, screaming, and whistling, threatening to bring down the centuries old walls. The band joined at the front of the stage, hooked their arms into each other's and took a deserving bow. They straightened their bodies, waved and then walked off the stage. The audience stamped their feet and hollered for more, but nothing brought the powerhouse band back.

Hurrikaine didn't do an encore.

As the curtains closed, Solange glanced over and sent Holly an encouraging look. No wonder everyone had been so anxious, the band not only played for their peers but jammed with them!

The stage lights dimmed, yet *Hurrikaine* did not return.

Solange leaned over and asked, "What do you think of your man? He's a better musician, performer, and entertainer than all those men who joined him on stage. He is why *Hurrikaine* is the most popular super band on the globe." She gloated.

Holly stopped thinking because she was on sensory overload. "I don't know?" she replied falling over her dry tongue. "I can't understand any of this. It's difficult to believe the man I've spent days with is that man ... Kaine. Who would believe him frolicking in rose pedals with me at the castle and picking lollipops?"

Then Michael, Chris, and Nicky joined the girls at the table.

Nicky trailed warning, "...prepare yourselves. History is about to be made."

Chapter Four

MY ONE AND ONLY

The wine-colored curtains opened slowly to reveal an empty stage, except for two bar stools and two microphone stands. A soft purple spotlight lit the simple setting. Ian entered holding an Ovation acoustic guitar and Kaine held Slick. Kaine sat casually without his suit coat. His crème-colored sleeves rolled up to his elbows, the waistcoat buttoned. He rested Slick on his leg like a respected old friend.

Holly's heart swelled with pride at the sight of her magnificent lover, the man that had made her the talk of the town. Holly leaned back, spine straight and crossed her ankles. She held her chin high with pride. She was the Heart of the *Hurrikaine,* and she wanted everyone to understand she loved Kaine always and forever. She smiled proudly. She was his lady recalling this incredible adventure started with their first kiss at the Hard Rock.

Kaine and Ian each hooked a heel over the bottom rung of the stools. The crowd jumped to their feet again, to cheer and applaud, pleased they had returned to entertain them. *Hurrikaine* never did an encore.

Both men adjusted their microphone stands to adapt to their instrument and then Kaine's to his voice.

Kaine slipped the strap on his shoulder and started to arppegiate on his guitar, embroidering a beautiful and delicate ballad. Ian joined the soul-filled melody on his keyboard.

Kaine took a deep breath and then spoke softly.

"All my life I've found music to be the way to reflect my feelings. I wrote this yesterday ... it's called, "My Lady.""

Holly's eyes burned, instantly swelling with happy tears as she watched Kaine close his loving blue eyes. He lifted his chin to sing with his one-of-a-kind, breathy, lonesome voice, so soft and angelic. The dim hue of the violet spotlight drenched him and made him appear enchanting, and inviting, as he called his audience near to hear about his love for Holly, deep inside his heart.

Holly barely felt Solange kick her under the table. She leaned over, never taking her eyes off her man giving minimum attention to Solange.

"I've never seen him do anything like this, he loves you so."

"It's so difficult to believe, Solange. But it's true, every exceptional moment," Holly confessed.

"Oh Kaine, I'll love you forever," she spoke in a whisper while her head nodded telling him she agreed with every word he sang.

Kaine, her precious one, sang his love song to everyone, so innocent, pure, and gentle, like his love for her. As it drew nearer its end, a great roar of the crowd swelled with applause, and then when the song ended Kaine and Ian rose to their feet. They stood like strolling minstrels lost in a timeless moment.

Kaine swung his guitar around on his back, and he bent at

his waist with Ian, long and gracious for their adoring audience. Together they stood straight, their faces filled with grace and humility. Then three guitar techs instantly descended on them, to relieve them of the guitar and keyboard.

Holly squirmed in her seat impatiently, wanting to hold Kaine in her arms and tell him how much she adored him for this once in a lifetime night. Kaine Walker, the reigning prince, cast her as the princess at the royal rocker ball. Kaine made all her wildest fantasies come true and so many beyond, with the whole world watching.

She smiled, graciously, helplessly lost in love with her man named Kaine.

Chapter Five

WHO LOVES YOU

The crowd yelled, whistled and stomped their feet. *Hurrikaine's* newest ballad would enter the charts number one. Holly reacted as if dumbfounded and unsure how to behave. She dabbed the joyous tears from her eyes. If she'd been pushed to describe her feelings, the only word that would come to mind was bliss. Kaine made his love for her immortal by writing "My Lady."

She sat with her back against the chair, her chin tilted up and the envy of every woman in the ballroom. She watched Kaine bow one more time, humbly accepting the audience's appreciation until he would take no more. Then Kaine held his hand up high for all to see. Eventually, the crowd quieted when they realized Kaine would speak.

Holly looked up to Kaine, and he winked at her. Confused, she wondered what would happen.

Kaine walked off stage left and returned with a huge bouquet of luscious blood-red roses, easily two dozens. Holly watched on in wonderment as Kaine stretched his free hand out toward her.

When the audience quieted, Kaine announced. "Ladies and gentlemen, please ... not for me, for my inspiration, Miss Holly Hill, the Heart of the *Hurrikaine*."

Holly wasn't sure what she heard and removed the earplugs quickly. What was he doing? The next moment Solange pushed her out of her seat.

"... go ... Kaine's calling you."

Kaine stepped away from the microphone coming for Holly. His fingertips magnetically touched hers, locking her in pulling her to him then beside him. Kaine stood in front of the microphone and proudly announced.

"This ... is My Lady."

He puffed his chest with pride and love oozed from his deep sexy voice as he laid the roses in her arms.

The crowd reached a frantic peak, and the deafening roar buzzed in Holly's ears. Kaine Walker surpassed all of her dreams and gave her so much more, his world and undiluted power fueled by his forever love.

The crowd chanted.

"Kiss her! Kiss her!"

Embarrassment burned her cheeks, but nothing like her hot passion rushing her body when Kaine's arms encircled her waist, luring her to him, covering her mouth with his soft, moist, kissable lips. She became deaf to the reactionary crowd exploding into frenzy.

A million miles away, locked in a kiss Hollywood would have been jealous of, Holly didn't want Kaine to move away, but he was and ready to release her. The scent of the roses crushed between them mixed with his cologne made her swoon. For a second she thought she would faint, but instead, she blindly followed his lead, curtsied while he bowed to the audience, then he clasped her hand and she followed him off the stage.

Kaine quickly led her behind a stack of amps. She placed the roses on top. How quickly she fell into his arms. She leaned against him, hoping he would see her passion for him flash in her eyes. She didn't need to coax him as her body meshed tightly into his curves. Their bodies were no longer separated, but one skin.

His words whispered into her ear stabbed at her as he gently reminded that she shared him with the world.

"Holly, dearest ... I don't want to leave you like this ... but I have to put in an appearance, at the very least a couple of hours. They expect me."

Kaine's wife, rock 'n' roll, demanded him, but so did she. She wouldn't let him go that easily. She had him for now. Nothing he said would change her mind.

"When I'm finished with you," she stated flatly.

Kaine didn't argue.

She sighed, glad he understood her message loud and clear.

Kaine pulled away, looked around, glanced down to her and she fell into his incredibly dreamy blue eyes that said he adored her with complete abandon.

"You win...." he confessed with a sigh and smiled at her with an equal dose of love and lust.

He greedily wrapped his arms around her waist, pressing her head hard against his chest. He spoke with the velvety voice of a man in love.

"My Lady, there are only a few times I've been scared. I mean genuinely terrified and right now is one of them. I can't imagine what I would do if I ever lost you. Promise me, we are forever love and you'll never leave me."

"I promise, forever love." She barely made audible because Kaine kissed her long, deep, taking her with him to bliss.

She surrendered to the swirling, spinning out-of-control, lost in his endless love as he spoke into her mouth.

"Right now I want to be inside you like I've never wanted so badly in my life."

He'd said it all.

"I want you. I need you too." She whispered back with a fading breath, kissing him back with the full intensity and fury of her love knocking him up against the stacked amps. Suddenly, the equipment crashed down, causing the roses to spread everywhere on the old stone flooring and in the midst of them laid his empty shoulder holster. She slid her arms down his back, releasing him suddenly, to snap back into reality.

"Where is your gun?"

"I gave it to Sarah to hold while I played."

Holly broke away.

"Sarah's … here?"

"Of course, she works for me." He reminded easily not understanding her concern.

"She's with me for all *Hurrikaine* business."

Well, this turned out to be a biting bit of news. Holly had forgotten the evil little bitch toured with Kaine. But before Holly gave Sarah more thought, Kaine took her hand and led her deeper into the musty darkness.

He took her far behind stacks of old trunks and crates. Hidden behind the barrier of their new world, a cord of silver light forced its way in with the fog and shadows from a cracked window. A break in the storm clouds allowed a thin sheath of moonlight to drop a thin beam of light to kiss Kaine's square jaw line.

She put the irritating thought of Sarah behind her because she became entranced in following the beam of light and leaving quick, moist kisses along his flesh.

Kaine took a deep breath, stepped away, and opened the trunk. He smiled, delighted to find a thick, timeworn wine-colored tapestry, and laid it out on the century's old, dusty stone floor.

Kaine held his hand out to her, palm up and the moonbeams kissed it.

He spoke softly. "My Lady Love?"

Holly placed her hand in his, accepting his offer.

He laid her down gently like a fragile porcelain doll. He followed her body line to lay close beside her.

She squeezed her eyes shut as if to forbid the harsh world of rock 'n' roll to come for him as if by shutting her eyes, she could ignore its contemptible existence.

Holly lay quietly.

Kaine draped his leg over hers and cradled her in his embrace. His warmth covered her body as his hypnotic scent consumed her. She eagerly anticipated his fingers to stroke her. To push her beyond this place called Bliss where she lived with him and she opened her eyes.

Spellbound she watched him part his lips to slide his tongue across the bottom. With the breathy, lonesome voice of the world's greatest singer the voice with no edges, he commenced singing to her softly, calming her, soothing her with her song "My Lady."

The silver moonbeams glisten on Kaine's lips while he sang to Holly in his language of love. He was making his music love with her, so private. He touched her heart in a most unimaginable way.

She listened to his open heart, convinced she would never, ever leave Kaine, no matter how fucked the times were. She stroked his face and played with the few stray cords of his shiny, dark hair. Her fingertips lingered, tracing the beautiful features of his magnificent face. She caressed his chest where the words of his love grew.

He understood her message of love to him. She needed to make love, long and lovingly, hard and soft, to show him her exploding love. She sighed, so overwhelmed, and pulled him to her, kissing his earlobe around the diamond stud while he continued to sing softly and sweetly like an angel in her other ear. Her head spun dizzily, more intoxicated by his pure love than all the cocaine and Cristal champagne she'd consumed.

Holly hoped to convince Kaine with the moves of her body to take her quickly. Then, her worst fear, far in the distance the sound of intruders. Panic leaped in her chest. She couldn't bear leave him, unable to be separated from her beloved.

She whispered. "I'm going to make love to you like you've never been loved."

"Marry me tomorrow."

"Marry you?" She gushed choking on her words.

"Yes. Why not? I have a job, a few dollars in the bank, my reputation is still intact, and you would make an honest man out of me." He teased, but then he wasn't.

Then with a serious tone, "I absolutely adore you and I promise to make you happy every day of your life."

He added a bit impatient. "Well?"

The dream man waited. He was waiting for her to say she would marry him. It was hard to think. She'd promised herself she'd say yes the next time he asked, This was Kaine surprising her, blowing her off guard, never able to predict his quicksilver behavior. She struggled with thoughts, then words.

"Paper. Don't we need papers?"

"Fuck. You're right, of course, counselor. But my lawyers can do anything. Then how about Paris? We'll plan to be married in Paris. That's three days from now. Thirty-six hours and you will become Mrs. Kaine Walker. That is if you're saying yes?"

"Oh, yes Kaine. I will become Mrs. Kaine Walker. There's nothing I want more in this world. The honor to be your wife, bare your children and raise a family with you, my love. Yes, yes! My Precious One."

"Do you think you might want to keep your maiden name for your sensational criminal cases counselor?"

"No. I think Holly Walker, Esquire sounds perfect."

"Great, it's settled. We will be married in Paris in three days and tonight we throw away the lollypops."

She smiled, her heart so open, so honored, her magnificent Kaine so close. "Babies, yes, my Precious One, tonight we start."

Kaine hugged her until she thought he would squeeze her final breath from her. He hummed the last verse of "My Lady" and then pulled back, gazing long and deeply into her eyes. His sexy, sultry, blue eyes told her how intensely he longed for her.

"Soon my love, soon," he promised.

"Three or four hours tops and we'll be back in our hotel

room where I can show you how you have made me the happiest man in the world. And I'm going to hold you to your promise, to love me, as I've never been loved before, My Lady. You can feel how much I want you now?"

She nodded yes. Kaine's rock hard love pressed against her belly with no mercy.

"I'm going to have to wait for a few minutes before I go out there. Listen to me and please, do exactly as I ask. I want you to go. Find Solange, stay with her and wait for me. I will be out in a few minutes, please?" His dreamy blue eyes begged.

Why didn't Kaine understand it was like ripping her heart out to be parted from him?

Her world started to spin out of control and nothing was right.

"Don't make me go. It's so cold without you...."

Chapter Six

DON'T YOU
(FORGET ABOUT ME)

Holly couldn't have anticipated the rush for Kaine's attention. He made his expected entrance and stepped off the stage before she told him anything, touched his hand or kissed his sweet lips one more time. His fans had sucked him into the black hole of rock 'n' roll.

The madness of his world had started.

Holly caught glimpses of Kaine searching for her across the sea of his admirers. There was no way to ignore this scene. This would be her life with a rock star. Her place would be the understanding second wife, patiently waiting for him while his adoring fans worshiped him.

Wife, incredible.

She let the smile grow until her cheeks burned with happiness. After a moment, the imposing crowd separated to allow Sir William Larchmont and John Roberts, in to congratulate Kaine. She barely saw the three men talking as she stood on her toes to catch a glimpse of Kaine. Eventually, Sir

William and John left the perimeter of the crushing crowd. When they vanished, the crowd filled the void, locking Holly out.

Solange circled the table, motioned to follow her and headed for the dessert table where any treat for the sophisticated pallet awaited. But Holly didn't think about food. The feelings of dread grew stronger. She needed to pull herself together, she was about to become Kaine Walker's wife. She held her chin up high and then took a breath and straightened her back. It was time to behave like the lady Kaine believed in and loved.

Solange stood companionably next to Holly.

"Here we are. Get used to it, the band will be signing autographs, posing for photos, and mingling for hours. Ian hate's it, he'd rather split and go back to the hotel and relax. I suspect for once Kaine feels the same way."

Holly retorted, "I can only think of taking him back to the suite and make wild and passionate love. Does that sound so selfish?"

"No, that's probably one reason why you're the Heart of the *Hurrikaine*. I must confess, it's the same with me. I've been here a few times but the all-star lineup has never been this impressive. The band worked hard for this night. Everything they have, they earned, and nothing came easy or was given to them. Each man is exceptionally special and talented, sacrificing everything to follow his love of music. And like you, I'd rather take Ian home because there's nothing like a live concert and an expressive audience, to get the love juices flowing."

Holly shook her head knowingly, so it was with rockers. Music and sex. And she had to laugh. It truly *was* sex, drugs, and rock 'n' roll. She remembered how sexually explosive Kaine had been with her after each performance.

She was impatient and didn't want to wait to get back to the suite to make love. She smiled, of course, there was the long car ride. Luka would have to find another way home.

Holly's thoughts were interrupted, overhearing someone ask a question.

"Who is kissing Kaine?"

The words instantly impaled Holly's heart, upsetting her more than she was willing to show on her face. She closed her eyes and gritted her teeth. "How can he?" Holly criticized aloud, dropping her head crestfallen.

"Part of the territory along with the tours, recording, the videos, the press. Everything is hard for everyone, but groupies are the worst for you and me. This lifestyle has many downsides. Fame is an overpowering force for anyone involved with it. No one should envy you or me. Kaine and Ian have the world. Kaine and Ian are our worlds."

Holly nodded her head in agreement.

"But look at it this way and hold on to it," Solange continued. "Kaine sang to you for over an hour and then to top it off, sang your love song, to *you*, for *all* to witness. I think your territory has been clearly marked. Even Luka sat back astonished at the lengths Kaine was willing to go to show his commitment to you. Luka was seething. Ian said no one told him about it because Kaine added the song at the last minute. That was one loud message he sent to Luka."

"Luka?" How was it they were back to talking about Luka? Holly changed the subject. "You're right Solange, about everything. Somehow, it doesn't help. I can't get to Kaine and I confess I'm filled with jealousy and spitefulness. It's making me hate myself and rock 'n' roll."

The overwhelming feelings of uneasiness ate at her guts. No way for a new fiancée to react and she was tired of complaining. She looked up and caught a glimpse of Kaine surrounded by his legions as the loneliness settled in like a shroud inside a coffin.

"Solange."

Holly turned to find Sir William and John in conversation with her.

"...wee, probably their best yet. Would you like to meet Kaine's inspiration? John Roberts, Miss Holly Hill," Solange said as she introduced her with a warm smile.

Smashing, to steal a term of Luka's, Holly thought. John stood next to her dressed handsomely in a tailored, dark-chocolate, tweed Asset suit, looking very distinguished. His bearded chin and collar-length hair a perfect complement to his handsome face, though he was not as tall as she'd imagined. But men like John always seemed larger than life.

"Brilliant, happy to meet you, Holly," he graciously added in a delicious British-accented voice, so smooth, so familiar. "You've added richness to Kaine's life."

Tongue-tied, Holly managed a simple. "Thank you."

John leaned closer to say something in Holly's ear over the loud voices surrounding him. She was distracted by his comment as her eyes locked onto Kaine's. She started to smile, but she did not find what she expected. His stormy black eyes pinned her, glowing with rage. She raised her eyebrows, wondering what was wrong.

John slipped his arm around Holly's waist for a second and pulled her politely to his side, avoiding a collision with a blinded waiter. John held her close until she regained her balance. Then he suggested in a brotherly tone. "Would you please come with me?" John placed his hand on her lower back, excused them to Sir William and Solange. John wove Holly through the dense crowd as everyone made a pathway.

Holly's mind raced, she fought the picture of Kaine's angry and intense eyes. And who had been standing beside Kaine smugly smiling? That bitch Sarah. What was happening?

John made small talk. "How do you like London? Enjoying the party?"

She answered without thought.

When John found a secluded area, he explained his reason for wanting to speak with her quietly. He shared a brief version of his history with *Hurrikaine*, especially with Kaine. He concluded his story. "I've known him for a long time and he's been alone too long. All he's had is music."

John laughed. His handsome face filled with a warm, comfortable smile and then proceeded to explain.

"Sometimes it's either your music or your private life. I hope, Kaine never has to choose between them."

She recalled Kaine's exact words in her hotel room.

I hope I never have to choose.

Holly was touched by John's depth of loyalty to Kaine. He was lucky to be surrounded by such faithful and sincere people. John's conversation tapered off as he spotted another of his many friends and excused himself.

But another took his place. She was at a disadvantage. Everyone knew who she was, her name and title — the Heart of the *Hurrikaine*. To her surprise, they all wanted to meet her, the mystery woman, the current girlfriend, or soon to be known as a wife. To her utter amazement, her new companion was the electric cowboy himself, Marc LeRouge, smiling at her.

"Is the mystery lady enjoying herself?" he sweetly asked. Marc was dressed semi-casual in a white shirt; the rest a black leather vest, coat, slacks, and boots, looking even more scrumptious in person. His kindness continued as he offered her a drink. He walked her over to the bar. A moment later, she stood gulping champagne. Her mouth was, so d-r-y. From over her shoulder, she inhaled an occasional gust of marijuana smoke floating past her from an open window.

Marc was easy, comfortable, firing off one anecdote after another about how he and Kaine were long time buddies, and wouldn't have missed Kaine's big night and jamming with him. As she was getting used to Marc's charm, and his flashing blue eyes proudly sharing stories with her about his children, he parted company only to have the flamboyant Joe Turner, joking and teasing her. He wanted to talk about who made her fabulous outfit. And every time she looked for Kaine, she found him in either another woman's arms or glaring at her.

Confused and disheartened, she drank another glass of champagne. One by one, the rockers of Friar Manor filled her card. Soon Kaine faded from her thoughts as she passed into the marijuana smoke filled corridors, to join new friends, to do things she'd never imagined. She inhaled lines of cocaine, secretly behind hidden alcoves, far from the bubbles of the finest champagne, and most importantly — Kaine.

Holly was alone no more. Everyone knew who she was, and she wore her badge well, the Heart of the *Hurrikaine*. It amazed her how they all wanted to talk to her, Kaine's mystery woman. All, except one, the red-haired bitch Sarah that stalked her with vicious green eyes. She turned away from Sarah and hopelessly drank from an always full, glass of champagne replenished by her onslaught of admirers. She was speeding out of control from one line of cocaine after another.

Holly lost all focus on Kaine and enjoyed socializing with the elite of the rock world. They came one after the other until she no longer kept the names and faces clear. She was overwhelmed and mesmerized by the heady guest list her feelings of dread became deaden by the alcohol and drugs until she finally believed she was safe.

It was then Holly recognized the familiar cool fingertips rake across her back. She smiled coyly. She'd wondered how long it would take him to come to her.

Holly turned and looked up into a pair of angel eyes. His soft, hypnotic voice so welcomed.

"I see you're doing bloody well."

"Luka...." she acknowledged so softly with a tiny edge of a slur.

His eyes sparkled, as they caressed her face and then dipped hungrily into her eyes, making her faint.

"Too much of everything," she confessed easily and leaned into him.

Run! She told herself.

Run as if he was the plague.

But he felt too good, too comfortable, and too perfect.

Luka smiled that familiar lazy, sexy smile of his. Cocked his head to the side in the boyish manner that said he was one hundred percent man and confessed. "I'd rather believe it was I that had this effect on you."

She raised her eyelids to look at him better. It was true, he did, and her eyes told him so.

"At lease, let me hold you up, Babe," he suggested as he tightened his grip on her back, holding her dangerously close and hcr lips an inch from his.

She lost herself in his fresh, sweet-scented breath.

Run.

Run. Before it's too fucking late!

Luka bent his finger and his cool knuckle stroked the hollow of her cheek.

She knew she wouldn't run, and she relaxed. She leaned the side of her head on his shoulder.

It was too late to run.

She'd already forgotten.

Her world started to spin. She relaxed her body following the curves of his, relieved to be locking everything out, and come to a screeching halt. Had he seen she wasn't able to keep everything together? That she'd needed to stop in his strong, competent arms?

Luka, so easy to look at, impossible to resist.

Luka seemed to be in a light-hearted mood, laughing, teasing, and shamelessly flirting with her. Kaine had been right. He didn't care if she was the Heart of the *Hurrikaine.*

Luka held her confidently, stroking her face and body, making her laugh at awful jokes.

Luka.

Mmmm.

Luka caught the attention of a waiter. Moments later, Holly stood drinking a cup of cappuccino with Luka he'd ordered especially for them. Her head cleared a bit in time to take on a new admirer, crooner Laurence Basil. Of course, he was joking with Luka as longtime friends, judging, by the way, that they swapped war stories. As the moments flowed into minutes, she found herself enjoying socializing with the always charming Luka and his never-ending list of friends. Laurence eventually went on his way and Luka quickly maneuvered her, back, far away from the prying eyes of the inquisitive crowd.

He was coming after her.

Run!

Which way?

To Luka … or from Luka?

He made up her mind, smothering her senses, squelching her good judgment, leaning her against the wall.

She knew what would come.

She relaxed.

She would let it come.

He looked at her, his eyes full of resolve and then it was too late. His need flashed brilliantly in his eyes and Luka placed his warm, succulent lips on hers, lightly at first as if to ask her permission.

Her body trembled in his arms but she did not shy away. It had been too long since she'd kissed him. And why not? Kaine had been out kissing girls for the sport as Luka called it.

Run.

But she didn't.

The cocaine and the champagne dulled her good sense, thrusting her further into his forbidden embrace. Luka's warm, strong arms surrounded her and Luka felt so good.

Better than good.

Perfect!

She was slanting her head, parting her lips, demanding his

kisses, kissing him deep, deeper still, in a manner she should have been ashamed of but there was no memory of why.

Luka had returned!

Run.

Why?

The muscles in his back tensed, Luka was holding back, letting her come to him and shower him with her passionate kisses. That admission instantly bit her, compelling her to pull away from him.

What was wrong? Luka did not attempt to kiss her again, but the sparkle in his eyes confirmed, that it was just a matter of time.

She nodded her head in understanding. Luka was taking his time, checking in to remind her she would never forget him, that he was always close by to help her.

How could she tell him he was wrong?

She would marry Kaine in less than thirty-six hours.

She loved Kaine!

What would that news do to her angel-eyed man?

The burning heat of embarrassment nipped at her cheeks.

Why was it so easy for Luka to manipulate her?

Holly met Luka's gentle gaze a second time. She wanted to break away from him, knowing she should. She must run away while still capable.

Luka continued to stare at her with his incredibly beautiful eyes.

The chemistry between them was brewing, starting to boil.

And when he spoke, his honesty blew her away.

"Kaine must be pleased with himself. He's so spoiled he thinks by writing a song for you and introducing you as his lady makes it true. I can give you everything he has and more. But, I refuse to buy your love. He's a foolish bloke, thinks all that fluff will stop me from coming after you. Keep me from loving you. There I've said it. I love you. Does it scare you? It scares the Hell out of him. Because he bloody well knows, you're in love with me too. And now I know it. Otherwise, you wouldn't have kissed me the way you did."

"No Luka, it's too much champagne, too much cocaine."

She trailed trying to explain.

"Are you blind to your own feelings? Wake up! Don't you understand? You're in love with me! Why else is it every time Kaine tries to checkmate me with you, you come to me, willingly, Babe, so willing? He knows this, and its twisting his guts. Your eyes glow like a lady in love when you look at me. Your body moves to fit me perfectly, saying it loves me. Your lips kiss me with passion as a woman deeply in love with me. I know it, others see it, soon the world will know. Bloody Hell! Babe, when will you know it?"

Holly shook her head to block his words. She couldn't listen to his words.

Luka was wrong.

She was about to become Mrs. Kaine Walker.

"Not true Luka. I'm... I'm going to marry Kaine ..., in Paris, in three days." There, she countered. Luka would stop.

Luka studied her, his eyes remained cool, the shade an icy blue. They look hardened and he narrowed his eyelids before he warned. "If you ever reach Paris."

His mouth crashed down on her like a man in love, fighting for her love, hoping to convince her. He demanded she realize that he was the one for her, not Kaine.

She surrendered her body to him, wrapping her leg around his, pushing her hips into his, and coiling her arms around his neck. She parted her lips to take all of his exploding love, so fierce, then growing into a tenderness she'd yet to experience from him. He crawled into her mouth kissing her deeply, clearing her mind of Kaine Walker, and taking her soul to keep.

Now he had everything but her heart.

There was no turning back, Luka Hunter always got what he wanted, and he wanted her, everyone said so, and as frightening as that news should have been, she was strangely at peace.

Luka kissed her for what seemed like forever, telling her he loved her a million different ways. How different the moment was. All her anxiety vanished after hearing his confession of *I love you.* It seemed right to have his hands touching her body wherever he wanted and she loved it.

He kissed her to oblivion and afterward he relaxed a bit, pulling her up to straddle his leg. He broke away. His love shimmered in the crystal, clear blue pools of his eyes.

A flush of arousal looked grand on Luka's face, long, straying, locks of his long, golden hair dripped down the beige Asset suit. The cloth hung on him perfectly, loose, familiar and like her, loved to be draped about him. His long blond hair was pulled back into a tail and there were many long golden strands feathered about his chin to caress his jaw line. A tiny gold earring hung delicately from his left ear, but he was no longer a beautiful pirate but her radiant Prince Charming.

Luka.

It was no use.

Luka had been telling the truth.

She'd never run from him again. And she hoped he had the

strength of decency to send her back to marry Kaine. Her betroth.

"Luka...." Was all she managed to say because she did love him in a strange and twisted way. She'd loved him since that first moment at the airport. But her gut feelings told her Kaine needed her more than Luka. Luka would survive. Kaine, she didn't know what her betrayal to him would bring?

"I see you're fighting with yourself. You do see I am right. You do love me. Now you know. I should pick you up and carry you out of here and never look back. But I can't bloody do that. You need to make up your mind and come to me. You need to stop letting Kaine, or I or anyone else, make decisions for you. You're an incredibly strong, capable woman, Babe. You can do this. I have everything but your heart and if you choose to give it to me, I won't be too far away."

"Oh, Luka ... don't."

"I realize, Babe. My confession of love is not as fancy as a song or magnanimous as announcing it in front of the world. I'm an especially private man, but I love you where it counts Babe, here in my heart. I love you enough to let you go. When you want me, I'll be close by, waiting for you because I can wait."

"Luka you're breaking my heart," she admitted once again stunned by the depth of his confession.

"You're my angel, my rescuer, my conscience, my beautiful dreamer. No one in my life has treated me the way you do. You make me stand on my own two feet, encourage me to try new things and as scary as that has been, I need you more now than I ever have. I don't have any idea what is right anymore."

"Yes, you do. You're a strong, intelligent woman and you've given Kaine all your power, your sensibilities. Listen to your heart. I believe you love *me* Holly Hill, and I can wait until you're sure."

Holly listened to Luka's name called. He looked over, turned his head and then back down to her. The same old look crossed his face, so sexy. He knocked her legs right out from under her. Would she ever get him out of her blood?

"Go, they need you now," she ordered, shaking her head wondering how everything became so fucked up again.

Luka flashed his beautiful, boyish smile, her vision of him blurred once again by his radiance. Luka pulled his hands from behind her back, took her face in between them, and kissed her firmly, but with restraint telling her to listen to her heart. And when he raised his head, he arched his crescent shaped eyebrows and asked.

"Are you the Heart of the *Hurrikaine*?"

Chapter Seven

HEADED FOR
A HEARTBREAK

Holly didn't have an answer. Luka walked away. That was an answer in itself. He threw his shoulders back. His spine straight. The center vents of his crème colored jacket flowed around his lean thighs while the loose strands of his golden hair were blowing in the gentle wind of his gait.

He never looked back.

Luka Hunter.

Holly exhaled a deep breath while shaking her head. Things moved too fast, and she still didn't have any idea what to do about him?

She reentered the grand ballroom, one hundred percent in love, a bit with Luka, but mostly with Kaine. She suspected that was not the place to be for a newly engaged woman.

Her body swayed as she bumped into people trying to maneuver the crowd, buzzed out of her mind. It was hard to focus, the room filled with smoke and the lights seemed dimmer than before. The track music blasted, and her head swirled with questions — but no answers.

"Where the hell is Kaine?" She bellowed mindlessly into the crowd.

A lingering thought of kissing Luka brought a warm explosion of feelings, to flood her heart. She sighed that definitely needed to be the last goodbye kiss. She must stay far away from Luka.

She looked, but everywhere she looked, — no Kaine.

The chill arrived.

Alone, confused and jealous, rock music wasn't fun anymore.

Infuriated, Holly searched the small groups of people until she located Kaine mister-center-of-attention. She pulled herself together and headed over to him as moving in as close as possible. However, she was prevented from penetrating the thick fortress because of groupies surrounding Kaine gushing all over him.

"Fuck!" she spat, following another rush of defeat.

Exasperated, she sat in the closest chair. How long would it be before she touched Kaine? Thoughts about how little she knew about him nagged at her, and that five short days ago, he'd been a complete stranger. She sat mulling over her doubts when a sharp grip on her upper arm turned to pain.

Holly stared up into Kaine's dark blue eyes that filled with fury and anger.

"Kaine!" The only word to escape her lips as he jerked her by the forearm, creating a great surge of biting pain.

He pulled her close to his face, his breath reeked of liquor.

The panic wrapped around her throat.

She shivered, knowing what to expect next when he was full of whiskey and cocaine.

His eyes accused her of horrible things. She shuddered, knowing what Kaine was capable of doing to her.

Chapter Eight

WICKED GAME

A terrifying chill blasted Holly. Her old companions fear and dread returned with lightning speed. She glanced around the room, buzzing on the cocaine and drunk from champagne.

She decided to keep her head clear to deal with Kaine in his present state of mind — definitely no more champagne and absolutely no more cocaine for her.

Kaine's thunderous voice demanded her full attention.

"Holly! Holly!"

Apparently, she didn't respond fast enough. Kaine's loud, deafening voice ruptured in her ear.

"Are you ignoring me?"

Her arm ached from his nail tips ripping the sheer material and then into her flesh. The stench of his liquor breath reeked causing her stomach to retch.

"Come with me," he slurred into her ear.

For the first time since she had met him, Holly was concerned about leaving with Kaine. But how to refuse him and not provoke a scene? The heat of shame flashed throughout her body, then stung her cheeks. Her calm behavior was vital to convince everyone nearby that turned to see Kaine's captive hold that nothing was wrong.

Kaine let go of her arm and lurched at her hand, missed, and snagged a jagged nail on her embroidered bodysuit. He tore a wide gash in the sheer cloth, slicing the delicate skin of her breast, drawing thin crimson droplets of blood.

The sacrifice had begun.

Stunned by the sting of her breast, Holly looked up, anxious by Kaine's erratic behavior.

His dark, blue eyes glared at her.

Between clenched teeth and with a quiet tone, he condemned her.

"Some fucking way for *my* girlfriend, oh, wait — fiancée to behave!" His voice dripped with sarcasm.

What did he mean? Whatever it was, the words were supposed to slap her with humiliation.

Apparently, because he'd said it under his breath, none of the party guests overheard him. Dizzy from his biting accusation, Holly instantly acquiesced to his demand to escape the party.

The crowd separated as he hurried her along, holding her hand and they didn't see him dictating her every movement as if a disobedient child.

What had she done to warrant his wrath? She was afraid to search his eyes for the answers.

Kaine pulled her down a narrow passageway, then another, then another, and finally down a dark, foggy and foreboding corridor.

Holly thought to resist but feared more punishment from

him. What was going to happen?

Kaine dragged her farther down the corridor.

Holly stumbled, losing her Prada heels, but he gave her no time to recover.

He jerked her deeper into the darkness until the sounds from the gathering were silenced except his heavy breathing.

A tiny wall sconce from another century scarcely lit the stifling dungeon no bigger than a jail cell. Her body trembled, and she squeezed her eyes shut. This couldn't be happening. She had to wake up, now!

Kaine pushed her up against the cold, brick wall, his face hidden by the black shadows.

Holly fought to block out his shrieking voice. Her face damp from the liquored saliva he spewed. She hadn't understood an audible word in his string of crimes against her. When he lashed out and grabbed her chin, the shadows revealed him glaring at her with menacing blue eyes.

"What the fuck did you think you would achieve flirting with John?"

John? When did she flirt with John Roberts?

Her mind froze, failing her, too dull from lack of sleep, the cocaine, and too much champagne. All she muttered in her defense in a soft, small voice.

"I don't know what you mean?"

"Don't hand me that fucking shit! Sarah told me about you flirting with John and like an asshole. I didn't believe her until I saw for myself. What are you trying to do to me? Make me out to be some kind of fool. In fact," he continued, "I saw you flirting with a long line of blokes."

He stopped and shook his head as if he couldn't make sense

and believe what he was about to say.

"And, let's not forget Luka!" He yelled, "I warned you about Luka. Holly ... I warned you. I fucking believed you were different Holly," he maintained, trailing off, looking away from her, disgusted, and still shaking his head.

The heart of the *Hurrikaine* stood shattered. But at least now, she understood the indictments against her. It was no defense, but she offered.

"Kaine, you kissed the women, so many women."

"I don't kiss them, Holly. They kiss me. I'm working, and you see they mean nothing to me. But that wasn't true when you were all over Luka. I saw with my own eyes Holly, how you felt, excuse me, feel about him. I saw you. He wasn't forcing you and you were so willing. Is it him you want?"

How to answer that? Of course, not, Kaine was her man, her lover, the man she'd agreed to marry. But she was too fucked up to think fast enough to defend her behavior with Luka.

The room spun and her head ached from Kaine screaming at her. But right now, her heart ached more. When she'd kept silent, she watched Kaine take her admission as rejection, that she no longer loved him.

Holly sank inside as his suffering raged in his dark, stormy eyes when he looked for her soul. But he did not find it because Luka took it with him.

She hoped for swift justice. Kaine would not take her betrayal easily.

He placed her face between his cold hands. His face etched with anguish moved closer. His lips crushed hers. The familiar taste of salty blood gushed into her mouth.

His heart was breaking, and she didn't dare attempt to stop

him and encourage more anguish or disillusionment. Dread filled her, sensing Kaine had only started.

The sounds of her distressed cries filled the chamber as Kaine swallowed each with kisses borne out of so much emotional pain. Not understanding his intentions magnified her concerns, but the heartbreak she experienced, knowing her behavior drove Kaine to this point devastated her.

His words from the castle returned to torment her.

> *You don't know what I'm capable of ... haven't you heard about what rockers do to groupies? You don't have any idea who I am. I could tie you up, or force you to do things many times ... many ways. I could thrash you senseless and I have enough money to keep it all quiet. Holly, you don't know who the hell I am. Though I don't mean to scare you, it's more of a warning. I don't deserve you, believe me. I'm no damned good for a sweet, loving lady like you. I am the man your mother and father warned you about…*

She recalled the last of that conversation.

> *I trust you, Kaine,* she'd claimed.
> He'd answered, *Maybe you shouldn't.*

But she did — still did.

Kaine broke from the kiss. He stared at her, looking for why he wasn't enough. Why didn't she love him?

Holly's tears streamed quietly and steadily.

She didn't want to think that he would hurt her. He didn't want to bring her pain. He loved her and she believed that. But her unforgivable lack of respect for him by kissing Luka was crushing him, bringing a pain so deep, she wasn't sure how he would respond to her. Would he give her more pain or love her so much that he would forgive her?

Her sobs grew louder.

Kaine planted his demanding mouth over hers again to silence her. For a split second, she thought the punishment ended, and Kaine returned to his senses.

For a second.

Then he pulled away.

"What the fuck do you have to cry about Holly? I've poured my guts out telling the whole fucking world you're my lady. I fucking asked you to marry me and have babies. How much more do you want from me?" He screeched inches from her face.

"I expect Luka to act like the bastard he is, but you, I trusted you to walk away. You want to be treated like the other women. I'll show you what it's like to be one of them."

He forced her down onto the cold floor.

"Take this fucking off, now! I'll fuck you so you'll never forget who I am."

She fought for words. Her mouth throbbed. Somehow, she had to make him see what he was doing.

"Kaine ... please ... not this way ... not like this...." Her voice trailed off into a silent plead as she stared into his black eyes.

It seemed as if Kaine listened to her pleas. His eyes searched hers, struggling to understand why she would betray him. Then in a breath's time, he changed his mind, pushing her down.

Request denied.

"No Kaine, no," she begged following a volley of screams.

She expected the worse.

Holly collapsed under him thinking if Kaine was to perform horrible things to her, so be it. But she wouldn't help him.

Holly quickly experienced his dissatisfaction as his harsh words lashed at her in disbelief.

"What? You won't do it for me? What is it? Luka? Should I fucking call Luka down here? And don't lie. You've always wanted to fuck him! I saw you tonight. I saw how passionately you gave him your sweet kisses. I saw your body wrapped tightly around his, already familiar with the rhythm of him. You were fucking him. Do you realize how worthless that made me feel? To see the woman, I'm in love with, asked to be my wife a few hours earlier, in Luka's arms — fucking him.

"You've wanted to fuck Luka since you met him." He screamed and then closed his eyes.

"Now you have and are Luka's whore. How could you Holly?"

Now she knew, who and why. And she knew when and where. But she couldn't tell him how. She didn't know how she could do that either. She couldn't bear the truth of his words.

How could she have indeed?

The moment certainly wasn't the time to point out it was a kiss, no more because he wouldn't believe her.

A cold, vengeful glare in Kaine's black eyes promised he wasn't finished.

"I should have listened to Sarah. She told me all along, you were nothing but a fancy whore. Said you were playing the two of us against each other. But I was a fool in love, wanted to marry you, cherish you, and raise children. I am such a fucking fool and I can't believe how blind I've been. Even in the end, I wouldn't believe her, until she took me to where she saw you disappear with Luka. There you were — hiding back in the shadows like the tart you are. You're Luka's and I will *never* trust you."

His face softened for a moment as if he were thinking of better times.

"I believed in you Holly, in our love together. I believed you were the one. Instead, you've betrayed me. Well, so be it, you're free to go to Luka. I can't be wondering if you're in the shadows betraying me with him. He can have you. He's won the fair damsel. The only problem, he's in love with a ghost that doesn't exist. When he realized you're not anything as sweet and pure as his precious Carrin, well, even he doesn't deserve to relive that pain."

She looked up into his beautiful, blue eyes that were filled with an unbearable agony. The truth of his tormenting pain rendered her mute.

Why did she betray him?

With Luka.

There's a limit with Luka.

She'd found it.

She exhaled a brief breath. Soon this assault would end. Kaine would take her body with force and give her his hate. She had no strength to fight him. It would be okay for then she would hate him too.

Dazed by the accusations, she closed her eyes while lying on the cold, stone floor.

Then like his namesake, the *Hurrikaine*'s mood changed. He dismissed his aftermath of the destruction. Kaine shook her commanding her to look at him.

Kaine gazed deep into her eyes, and he caresses her cheek with all the tenderness and compassion she'd grown to love in him.

He looked up to the centuries old walls and closed his eyes for a moment, then looked back down to her. She saw it in his eyes, all his forever love for her and the tears that welled there.

Kaine tenderly slipped his hand under her head, supporting it gently with his hand. He pulled her face near his. A single, warm tear dropped on her cheek. Kaine bent his head and kissed her lips, lovingly, sweetly. Then he backed away and spoke in a tone of resignation, she never wanted to hear again.

"Goodbye, My Lady Love. I'm sorry you don't love me. Tell Luka, I'm sorry for him. And if you must — tell him that I still love you, probably always will. You're My Lady Love, and your love damn near destroyed me tonight. But even he doesn't deserve you."

Kaine moved away to stand up and then straightened his back.

Holly wanted to reach out and grab a hold of Kaine's arm, to tell him to stop. She'd never considered it would be Kaine to leave her. He'd promised. How was she to explain she did love him, the forever love?

However, what he'd said was true. She didn't understand the twisted turns in events any better than he did. But he'd been kissing the women too, the long days and nights of too much cocaine and alcohol.

And then Luka.

After all the pain and confusion, she didn't have a clue about what to do about Luka.

There was too much to explain, and she didn't have the strength. In those agonizing moments, she decided to let Kaine go. He was suffering too much from hopelessness and heartbreak, but mostly from her devastating betrayal, to hear her words. She watched the back of his suede shoes weave off down the corridor, leaving her behind in a pool of misery, leaving her behind, without her Precious One.

Holly lay quiet for a few seconds, thankful she had weathered the wrath of his crushed heart. A quick survey said she bore her own broken heart, and the searing guilt of betrayal, but she'd survived the landfall of the *Hurrikaine*.

Holly rolled over to flatten out on the cool, hard floor, drifting, crying her heart out unaware if seconds or minutes passed. She twisted to lie on her side and then closed her eyes.

She never saw the black shadow moving closer to her.

Chapter Nine

HERE COMES TROUBLE

Holly didn't see the black leather boot that crashed into her ribs. She didn't see it coming for her twice with such force that it caused her to coil up into the fetal position to stop the excruciating pain.

She tensed all her muscles hoping to stop the sting on her face from the gloved fist that made her head bounce up against the concrete wall, twice. Each time it bounced, it sent a fresh wave of stabbing pain in her head. Her clothes were ripped from her body. Her tuxedo pants pulled off and thrown beside her. Then something spilled over her. Seconds later, she inhaled the rich, sensuous scent of roses. Green, hate-filled eyes, moved closer to her and long red hair, fell on her face. The cold nozzle of the gun was pressed hard on her cheek. She heard the hammer of the gun pulled back, then the click of the trigger.

The chamber … empty.

Hideous words spilled with a crisp British accent.

"I told you. You're fucking history bitch! Next time you get in the way of Kaine and me, I'll use this gun and you can count on all the chambers loaded. I will kill you bitch with Kaine's gun. If you know what's good for you Princess Bitch, you won't mention our little meeting here, to anyone. I've taken the clothes off your back so you have no way to go back to the gathering. Go, be the repulsive bitch you are, take these roses Kaine gave you and crawl back in the hole you came from. Or, like tonight, next time you won't see me coming and I won't leave you alive."

"With the way, Kaine and Luka have been at each other's throats over you, guess who will spend the rest of his miserable life in jail for your murder?" her vile voice threatened and then laughed.

Holly fell the foot kick her thighs, again, and again until she dropped off the ledge of pain into darkness.

It was impossible to judge the loss of time. Holly turned over and pain shot throughout her body in every direction like fireworks exploding. She forced open her eyes to glance down the dark corridor.

Alone.

Her first thought was to find a way to maneuver down the ominous corridor, to leave this dungeon where the destruction of the *Hurrikaine* made landfall. But she was drifting helplessly in and out of dreams and illusions, unable to distinguish the difference as she lay on the cold floor of the corridor.

Eventually, she was conscious long enough to summon strength and sit up, placing her back against the cold wall. She willed herself to stand. She touched her face and there was blood smeared all over the back of her hand when she brought it into view. The intolerable pain spread evenly throughout her body. She didn't attempt to stand and focus at the same time, and instead, closed her eyes to stop the dizziness and nausea.

She slumped back down the wall, caught her breath, and decided to crawl. She put one hand in front of the other pulling torn muscles. Pure will forced her to move gradually down the corridor to where it joined a larger, better-lit passageway.

There she sat and rested, wiping away the continuous stream of tears and took inventory. She discovered she only wore bits and pieces. The tuxedo pants were gone. The thong barely covered her, her body suit ripped away from her chest, making it impossible to reenter the ballroom.

A grievous pain tore into her frayed body as she cautiously braced herself against the wall and glided up the smooth surface. She straightened her legs and staggered along the faded, peeling wallpapered corridor, passing room after empty room, stumbling ahead lost, alone and broken.

She pushed her bruised and battered body forward one small step at a time but the torment of her heart — a shattered heart, was worse than the pain in her body. She had lost her Precious One. Whatever her crime, it had been too grievous.

He no longer existed to love her.

As she limped along, she worked out a plan. She had to find clothes, locate a phone to call a cab, collect her passport and credit cards from her hotel, then straight on to the airport, and catch the first fucking plane out of London to anywhere.

Hot tears continually forced themselves to stream down over her cheeks.

Luka's words came to her.

If you choose to give me your heart, I won't be far away.

Where the hell was Luka?

How was she to justify her unfaithful and traitorous behavior to Kaine when there was no logical way to explain

Luka to herself? Kaine caught her in her indecision. Everyone warned her it would be dangerous. And it was. She cursed herself, acuity aware of exactly how all of this had this happened.

But all that tapped away in her head, loud and clear was…

I'll use this gun, Kaine's gun to kill you. Guess who will spend the rest of his life in jail for your murder.

Whose voice was that?

Holly shivered at the memory of the cold steel of the muzzle, of Kaine's gun, pressed against her face. Hot tears flowed again, and steadily. She reeled in the aftershock but chose to push ahead, quietly, melting into the dark shadows until she arrived at another junction.

Her head pounded, her body shivered from shock deep, down in the cold, damp manor. Disoriented, her vision gave her moments of concern.

Still, she didn't have any idea which direction the main hall was or even where in Hell she was?

She closed her eyes.

Darkness claimed her.

Chapter Ten

VICTIM OF LOVE

The scent of his fresh breath suddenly consumed her. She grabbed quick, life-saving breaths as if she was underwater and out of air and he was the only lifeline.

Holly barely saw him. Tall and brilliantly handsome, taking her into his arms. He pressed his soft, warm lips to her cool cheek, whispering sweet words she was unable to understand while trying to kiss away all her pain and torment. He whispered to her to hold on to him.

She sank deeper and deeper into dreams and fantasies.

Holly tried to move forward and nuzzle the warmth near her face. She moved closer to the light brush of a smooth, warm hand stroking her face. She slowly opened her eyes. Her vision remained blurred, but she recognized the beautiful baby blue eyes-to-die-for. They were filled with worry and something else.

"It is okay Babe, I've got you. I'm going to pick you up and take you out of here as I bloody should have earlier. I have a car waiting out back."

Holly couldn't think — couldn't argue. Twilight recaptured

her as she allowed her bruised and battered body to be lifted. The riveting pain followed every movement. But everything was all right. Luka had her.

Holly faintly overheard Luka swearing.

"I'll get that bastard for this."

That's what she'd seen in Luka's eyes, retaliation, and then revenge. His strong arms held her closer to him. Even in her delirium, she wondered where he'd been.

She babbled. "I've been looking for you. Said you'd be close by … where … were you? It hurts so much to breathe."

Luka spoke with a soft, assuring tone.

"I won't leave you again. I swear it."

"Good." She managed to whisper.

Luka was there.

Safe. All she wanted was him near as he placed her in a sitting position in a car. Luka carefully propped her up and then covered her body with something warm. He closed the car door and started the motor.

It was cold.

Her head spun in circles and she couldn't distinguish any sounds other than the pounding in her ears until the sweet sounds of Kaine singing "My Lady" reached her ear. The love-laced words of his song wrapped a warm, protective cocoon around her mind and memories. She envisioned Kaine stretched out beside her somewhere together in forever love.

The black rain unmercifully beat down on the windshield. A battalion of red-tail lights fought to escape the hellish manor, leaving Luka trapped in the bottleneck driveway. He sat patiently, waiting for his turn to leave. He never said a word, but she heard the grinding of his teeth.

She slowly opened her eyes and barely recognized the monstrous manor. A loud commotion at the side doorway drew Holly's dazed attention. She looked up to see the tall, dark shape of a man, stumbling, held upright by a red-haired woman. The man slumped on the diminutive figure.

They looked familiar.

A crack in her memory allowed the words.

You're history bitch.

A fresh rush of anguish flooded her. Bits and pieces flashed in her mind. More fragmented pictures came to her.

Kaine.

The corridor.

His accusations.

His kiss goodbye.

Sarah.

What did it all mean?

Holly watched on as Sarah spotted her sitting in the car.

Sarah went up on her toes to kiss Kaine. He reciprocated in a disgusting and drunken manner.

Holly quickly glanced away.

All that filled the cab of Luka's borrowed car were the lonesome wails of her shattering heart.

Hot tears filled her eyes, quietly spilling down her cheeks.

"Luka, take me out of this Hell as quickly as possible," she insisted in a forced whisper.

"To Kaine?"

Holly had been to the eye of the *Hurrikaine,* and there she'd discovered the exquisite pleasure and excruciating pain.

Now, she wanted out.

"Never again."

Chapter Eleven

HARDEN MY HEART

Holly didn't notice the silence. The fuzziness in her head was difficult to clear. Too many glasses of champagne and too many lines of cocaine had her reeling.

She didn't recognize she was drifting in and out of a chemically induced blackout.

The heat in the car was inviting, and she looked down to see Luka had draped his coat over her shredded clothes. The tracks of her blood were imprinted on the lapel of the light-colored coat. Her black evening bag lay in her lap.

"What would I do without you? Thank you for rescuing me," she whispered.

"I don't deserve your thanks. I should have prevented this," Luka said evenly as if to hold his anger in check.

She watched the muscle of his jaw twitch. The knuckles of his fingers were white as he gripped the steering wheel. She wasn't sure what to say. It seemed they were in a two-seat sports car. The color lost in the black, foggy night.

Holly reached out with her right hand to touch Luka's thigh, to show him her appreciation. The movement seemed so unnatural sitting on the opposite side of the car, yet how natural it was to rest her hand on his thigh.

"I won't ever let Kaine hurt you again, Babe."

"I'm sure you won't, Luka."

She leaned back, knowing he spoke the truth. The events of the evening were hazy at best, with long stretches of blank time. Even the corridor was becoming sketchy and wondered if it ever happened. She understood she'd suffered terribly and for some reason was responsible. It wasn't clear why. She would ask Luka another time. Soft blues music poured from the car speakers lulling Holly to a renewed comfort zone. Luka inched along because of the impenetrable fog surrounding them. The first hazy lights Luka came to he stopped.

"What's here?"

"Hopefully, something to drink to warm you while I check in to see if the private surgeon has arrived at a secret location. I can't take you back to your hotel in this condition."

Without missing a beat, Luka pulled out a vial.

"No, thanks," she insisted. "I've had enough illegal drugs to last me a lifetime."

"Ah, come on Babe, fuck 'em! You don't have to let Kaine get the best of you, do you? You are your own woman, aren't you? This is cocaine. A drug. A pain killing drug. The best money can buy. It will take the pain away." He assured.

She wasn't sure she wanted to forget this pain.

"You're never out of cocaine are you?"

"My sworn duty to please." He winked.

"Thanks, but no thanks."

"As you wish." He declared obeying her demand.

They were in the thick of an impossible fog and unable to

see to the end of the car's hood. She opened the door to put her weight on her thighs and tried to stand. No good, it was a toss-up, which muscle hurt most.

"Stay put," he demanded and disappeared.

She drifted into nothingness and then he returned with two giant mugs filled with steamy tea and a bag tucked under his arm. The warm liquid seeped in gradually and felt incredibly soothing. It calmed her shattered nerves and warmed her freezing hands.

"Ice in the bag is for your head, brandy in the tea is for your heart," he instructed and then started the car.

"Eaten anything in the last twenty-four hours?"

"I can't remember, can't remember...."

"Make sure you eat today if you can't remember that means it's been too long."

The rush of the gentle caffeine cleared more of the fog from her head. She learned quickly to obey her body. If she breathed shallowly, it alleviated a great deal of the pain.

Luka went on about something, but she wasn't listening. The shock was wearing off and more and more of the grim details returned to her. A blistering sorrow flooded her heart followed by an intense guilt. All she was able to identify was empathy, and seemingly for Kaine's pain, but there was no memory as to why he was in pain. But then an unrelenting guilt stabbed at her. It was true. She had betrayed him in a most callous, and unforgiving manner she would have never believed of herself and had done it in front of everyone he loved and respected. Her tears flowed again. She was sure this was why it's called a bleeding heart because it literally hemorrhaged.

A chill passed through her. She pulled Luka's coat tightly

around her chest and the masculine scent of Luka quieted her at once. She touched the back of her head and found a giant goose egg. It throbbed when she touched it. She reached into the bag and pulled out chopped up chunks of ice, protected by a plastic bag. She applied it and looked over to Luka.

He glanced back. The blaze of revenge in his eyes said Kaine Walker was going to suffer.

"I must look a sight," she said.

"You're beautiful," Luka nodded and smiled gently.

"You look like you've had a rough night, but you're always beautiful. I cleaned up your face, and other than wearing a thong and my dinner jacket which is my personal favorite, you look smashing."

She forced a smile encouraged by his sweet words. She looked at her reflection in the window. Luka was right. She didn't have the facial bruises expected after her ordeal. But her ribs ached.

What the hell happened?

"What the hell happened?" Luka asked sharply.

"Did you say something?" Holly questioned, looking at Luka with a puzzled expression.

"Yeah, you said, 'what the hell happened?' I wondered what you meant. Are you ready to tell me?"

"What I can remember is hazy."

Holly unraveled bits and pieces of her trip to ecstasy and terror at Friar Manor.

"...and he screamed you told him I was flirting with John Roberts and the others!"

"That's not what I bloody well said. That's what his fucked up jealous mind invented. I said John liked you and so did everyone else. I thought the news would put him at ease and please him that you were well received. What's not to like, you're beautiful, sweet, level headed and unaffected? An impossible combination to find these days," he praised and flashed an affectionate wink.

"I'm no longer unaffected," she snapped defensively and continued to unravel the bits and pieces of memories of her tale of torture.

"He what? Threw you up against the wall and ripped off your clothes? I wondered … I'll get that bastard."

Luka's tone and hostile words frightened her.

She saw the venom shine brightly from his eyes that he meant every word he spoke.

"I have ways," he added.

Yes, she was sure Luka did. But she didn't want Kaine injured. Holly simply wanted a plane ticket to L.A. and left alone to heal.

And oh yeah, never hear the word *Hurrikaine* again!

But Luka continued. "Kaine has always had a volatile temper. I'm bloody glad I had found you before he actually hurt you."

"If I remember correctly, he'd finished with me long before you found me. It's hazy, but he left me to crawl out of that dungeon of horrors. I think I remember the red hair of that fucking bitch, Sarah. I remember she had something to do with it. She was down in that hellhole, I'm sure of that. If I *ever* see that bitch, again, I'll scratch her fucking eyes out. In fact, I'm pressing charges. Assault and battery with a deadly weapon."

"Babe, hold on, you can't."

"Can't? Yes, I can!" Holly admonished, incredulously.

"Babe, I'm glad to see you're not in pain and I understand your need for revenge but think. If it got out to the press what happened between the two of you women fighting over Kaine? The press would have a field day not to mention how they'd hound you. Think. You're mad and hurt now. Revenge does sound sweet. Believe me, I agree. But when the press was finished, grinding you down you'd be in greater pain. That's why I'm taking you to a private surgeon. One I can make sure won't become an anonymous tip to the press. You can't handle the press in this beaten condition."

His words made sense, but her emotions wanted blood — Sarah's.

"You're right, of course, Luka. I can't take much more of anything." She hated to admit to herself it was killing her to be away from the gentle man she'd fallen in love within the music video.

"So what else happened?"

"Luka I can't talk to you about Kaine. This is wrong."

"That's another reason I love you, Babe, you have a conscience. Something most of us lost many years ago. But it's okay. I don't expect you to turn off your feelings for Kaine any more than you did with me.

"This has become one hell of a mess since I first saw you at the airport. I think I wanted to love you then, only I didn't want to believe it was possible. The night at the Hard Rock when you left with Kaine, it changed something in me. I've never cared about Kaine, or his women though many would argue the point. But you were different. You'd given me something I hadn't had in a long time."

"What Luka?" she questioned, dropping her hand to rest on

his hand gripping the gearshift.

He glanced down and then quickly up to her. His beautiful eyes sparkled as he said one word.

"Hope."

"Hope to experience real feelings again. Hope that I might be able to give love to another human being. Hope, one day I'd have the things a man dreams of sharing with a woman, love, commitment, family. I'd hoped I could be loved again. You gave me that Holly."

She was dumbfounded. "I never realized."

"It took me a long, lonely night to understand it too. At first, I was like everyone else. I assumed these feelings were about the old competition Kaine, and I devised to keep from going out of our minds with the tedious boredom of touring. Soon I realized it wasn't that. Kaine and I hadn't seen much of each other the past four years and we'd both grown up a bit. To his credit, I believe he did fall in love with you, as I did, as I believe you did with me."

"It's true Luka!" Holly dared with excitement.

"I did fall in love with you, possibly at the airport, or when I found myself in your arms outside the pub. Because when I discovered you backstage at Wembley, I was making plans to seduce you, something I hadn't done in so many years. I don't understand why Kaine became involved. How can I love both of you so intensely?"

Holly looked up hoping to obtain his wisdom, to shed light on this horrible turn of events. Instead, she found him smiling. Was she losing it? Why was he smiling?

"What?" She retorted, impatiently.

"It's good to hear you say you've been in love with me from

the outset at the airport." He glanced at her, smiled his sunny Luka smile. He was striking, even when his eyes were tired and his face worn with the lack of sleep and worry about her. She reached out to stroke the day's growth of beard that hugged his face and her fingers caressed his long hair that lay disheveled around his shoulders.

Yes, it's possible she had loved Luka all along, and what sort of hell had she put him through? She placed her hand briefly on his cheek. He glanced back to the road, kissing her fingers when he moved his face.

"There must be something else we can talk about," Holly suggested, hoping to change the subject because she didn't want to take on more guilt over how horribly, she'd treated Luka.

He inched the car through the dense fog for a long time.

Silence. He was lost deep in thought.

When he spoke aloud, he inquired. "Are you aware that Kaine signed into a rehab clinic four years ago and has been clean and sober since then? That is, until three days ago, something's triggered all this."

"Well." Holly sat back, trying to absorb this new information. "Why on earth have you been supplying him with all this cocaine?"

"I'm not his keeper. He's a big boy. Besides, at the castle, he told me to bring him cocaine and keep it coming. Since I'm here to film him until after the Paris concert, it's my job to keep him happy. My suspicions are, he was not sleeping enough to keep up with his responsibilities, or his time with you drug up major nightmares, or unresolved issues as the pop psychologists would say."

"Is this supposed to explain why he became so insanely

jealous over my conversations with John and the others?"

"Oh, especially John, because one old girlfriend wanted to shag John while he was working on a project with Kaine. Everyone watched Vicki that was her name, flirt, and tease John though I don't think John gave her a second look. She kept making a fool of Kaine, took joy in jabbing him with painful remarks and longing looks at John."

Kaine's words echoed from the corridor — *make me look like a fool.*

Luka continued, "I thought he was over Vicki. She was mental." He acknowledged as he shook his head.

Holly didn't notice she was sucked back into the *Hurrikaine's* history and asked, "What about that fucking Sarah? What's she to Kaine?"

"Babe, you're using profanity," he chuckled.

She was so glad to see that sunny smile of his, she'd missed it. She squeezed his thigh, running her hand up and down his lean muscles, so glad to be back with him, surrounded by love and safety.

"Sarah's … his lapping dog, to put it bluntly. She's been around since the early years. Unfortunately, I've known her since I was a lad. She lived on my father's estate. Her father was the groundskeeper. In fact, Sarah introduced me to Kaine. She's always picking up the pieces, especially after Vicki left. He is seldom civilized to Sarah, but she stays, puts up with him. She calls it love. I call it sick. After the rehab clinic, to repay her for years of loyalty he hired her to take care of him. He refers to her position as 'personal assistant' but it's more like a wife without any benefits. He won't let her get any closer than her knees if even that anymore. She waits for him to call."

"How pathetic," Holly snarled.

"Welcome to rock 'n' roll," Luka chortled.

"I wouldn't blame rock 'n' roll for Sarah's fucked up delusions. But it's goodbye for me. She can have him."

Suddenly, Kaine's words echoed in her head.

He can have you.

The words made her heartstrings tug for Kaine. Kaine had trusted her enough to love her again, in spite of Vicki and her betrayals. She'd crushed him too because he believed she'd betrayed him like Vicki? Only this time with both John and Luka? Could she blame Kaine?

Holly pulled up the blanket Luka had spread over her lap. Her arm throbbed, and she remembered more bits and pieces of Kaine in the black corridor.

"What Babe, your face seems pained. Need something?"

"No, thank you." She poured a sip of brandy into her empty mug, leaned back thinking that she was hurting deeply inside because of Kaine. She needed to harden her heart and shake the morbid thoughts from her mind.

"I can't wait for peace and quiet, mostly to soak in a hot bath."

"Soon Babe, soon," Luka promised soothingly and then lightly placed his hand on her thigh.

She wove her fingers through his.

The cold, bleak morning before the dawn's early light surrounded her. She was glad for Luka's love and support. She glanced at him, his shirt was wrinkled, splatter with her blood. Apparently, she was doing better because she wondered about what she was going to do with Luka. But was it possible to confess to loving him with a pure heart? And then she Kaine's words arrived.

E*ven he doesn't deserve you.*

What had she done?

Who was 'he'?

Holly dropped her chin to her chest. Whatever it was, it had been unforgivable. She needed to catch a plane, go home, and never return Luka's phone calls in L.A. He'd do all right there. Every woman in L.A. would be after Luka Hunter. Eventually, he would find a woman to love him as he deserved. She was no good for either of these two men. Perhaps she would accept Brett's proposal. She fit his expectations of her. Perhaps they were a match after all. She wiped away sorrowful tears and looked over to Luka thinking he was wonderful.

"We're here," Luka announced stopping alongside a row of houses.

They were all the same and she was unable to tell where one started and the next one ended. He came around to help her out of the car. She noticed beautiful Luka, standing under the street lamp.

Holly quietly shook her head. She'd no time for lustful thoughts. She gingerly stepped out of the car into Luka's waiting arms. It would be impossible not to think of him.

When they left the doctor's office, she was doing much better. The doctor gave her a potent shot for the pain and given Luka the option to wrap her bruised ribs if she needed it. Miraculously, x-rays showed no broken bones. She suffered from a slight concussion and fragmented memory, due to the cocaine and alcohol ingestion. However, the doctor predicted she would be understandably sore for a few days. He'd instructed Luka to apply ice to the back of her head and to let her soak in a hot tub as often as she wanted.

To silence the doctor, Luka peeled off a cash payment from the top of a thick stack of English notes.

He shrugged his shoulders. "I have to pay him more than the rags will to keep this quiet." Luka cheerfully volunteered to monitor her and to note any temporary disorientation by watching her carefully for the next forty-eight hours until she left for L.A.

Luka took her back to her suite at her old hotel figuring the paparazzi would never look for her there. The hotel lobby was deserted when the concierge handed her a card key, smiled as if he was glad to see her again since she'd been in such a hurry the last time there with Kaine.

The painful memory momentarily wrenched her heart.

Other than that, the concierge didn't bat an eye over Luka's blood-stained shirt or her wearing nothing but his blood-spattered coat.

Luka held her tightly, and she rested her head on his shoulder as they rode up in the elevator. Holly passed a security man placed outside the elevator's door. She glanced up to Luka.

"I called in support while you were with the surgeon, for protection in case there was trouble. You're safe now. Kaine cannot get to you. No phone calls, no visitors."

"Surgeon?"

"What we call the doctor."

She nodded, understanding.

"You think of everything." This was good news. The doctor's shot put her in a euphoric mood. Holly placed the card in the door and she turned to face him while Luka slid his arms around her. She naturally folded into the curves of his body.

Safe in his embrace, he gently kissed her lips. His breath smelled sweet, his lips soft, tender, but mostly comforting. The gash on her lips smarted, reminding her of Kaine and rendered her unable to pretend.

Luka pulled away, looked down at her, his icy-blue eyes filled with devotion she didn't deserve. She didn't respond because all she experienced was an outstanding twisting of sorrow mixed with deep remorse for her lost lover.

Luka spoke first.

"Forgive me. I swore I'd wait until you gave me your heart. I will. I'm acting selfishly. Especially, after all you've been subjected to, Babe. Please, say you forgive me?"

"The kiss was kind. I need to remember that most people are not cruel. Kaine was right about you. You do care for me. You've rescued me again. And I'm positive you will keep this disgusting, sordid mess out of the papers.

"Forgive you?

"Come inside Luka, you need a well-deserved rest," she tested and squeezed his hand.

Chapter Twelve

FOREVER

Holly blundered into the darkness of her hotel room. She remembered where the furniture was placed and headed straight for a silk settee. Luka bustled past her to enter the bathroom. Soon there was the sound of water flowing, filling the tub.

She settled in and then realized any sudden movement caused bone-jarring pain, but other than that, the shot was suitably effective. She pulled a vial out of Luka's coat pocket. She placed it on the table with the other bottle Luka had squeezed into her hand as he'd driven to the hotel, *in case you change your mind,* he had said.

Luka came out. "It's ready, Babe. Let me help you."

His usually brilliant eyes were pink, sad, rimmed with the sharp edge of revenge. He'd rolled up the sleeves of the pale blue shirt smeared with blotches of her blood. Even his expensive beige trousers had blood splattered all over them both never to be worn again. She shook her head, what happened?

She trembled again.

"Don't worry." He persuaded to calm her. "We'll get beyond

this. Let me help you. This won't be the last time I hold you in my arms naked, especially if I have anything to do with it," he teased and smiled.

But the usual sexy curl didn't wrap around his lips. His soothing attempt to put her at ease hadn't worked on her either.

"It won't be the last." She lied with a thin veil of shame, but she was sure, this was the last time.

Holly reached out for him.

"I'm so sorry. If I'd only stayed with you, none of this would have ever happened."

Luka came closer, oh so close, enough to see his eyes warring with himself. He swallowed, trying to restrain his need and instead give her comfort. He quickly looked away and took her by the hand to help her up gently to stand. He peeled off the last of the thong and unzipped what was left of her body stocking. She would never have believed what it would take to find herself with Luka again, wearing nothing.

Her heart leaped into her throat and she asked, "How long did the doctor say I would be sore?"

"Maybe a few days, let's see how you are after a long soak in the tub?"

She didn't argue. Her head spun. She sat.

Luka's cellular rang. He answered edgily. "No! You take care of him. I'm unavailable! No. I'll call when I'm on my way. I don't know how long, dammit! Can't you bloody well do anything?" he yelled and then pushed the button off, pushed the antenna down and set it on the table with a loud thud.

She looked at him wanting information, but too afraid to ask.

"It's Kaine, he's...." Luka's voice filled with fury, his eyes flashed with a thirst for revenge.

"I don't want to hear," she said and shied away from Luka.

"Don't worry Babe. I'll get the bastard!" He roared, the vengeance flowing freely.

"Luka, don't hurt Kaine. It won't help me."

Why did she think Luka would listen to her? Her words would never convince him. His eyes narrowed, no doubt steeped in thoughts of retaliation. They told her Kaine wouldn't win this time. A violent gust of wind blew against the windows and punctuated the moment with a frightening crash. Hadn't the destructive storm and madness passed? She hoped it had.

Luka turned, and she saw him standing in the dim lighting. It had been too long since she had seriously looked at him. But it was as if she saw him for the first time. Warm, comfortable memories with him flooded her, and she remembered those first hours when she'd met him in Chelsea — her handsome stranger — Luka. The ease of the memories brought a tear to her eye. She did love Luka so.

"No Babe, you can't look at me with those eyes ... like that. Relax. Let me take care of you." Luka coaxed with that sexy expression, knowing a woman wouldn't dare say no.

"I want to see what that bastard's done to you."

Too weak to do for herself, she gave in letting him care for her.

Luka knelt down on one knee, helping her to stretch out on the settee. A moment of modesty washed over her and slipped her hands up to cover her bare breasts.

"The doctor's prognosis was; mostly bruises, and a few superficial lacerations," she weakly explained.

"Lie still. Let me judge for myself." He muttered curse

words and his face wore a grim expression. He briskly ran his warm hands up her cool leg as his fingers probed her sore muscles.

She yelped.

"Sorry." He apologized under a whisper. "I'll be gentler."

Luka's hands moved higher, his fingers fanned as he touched her lithe thighs. His touch was soft, gentle, and fiery. His touch wasn't like at the doctor's, sterile and removed a wounded body to be evaluated.

Luka's eyes followed his hands. She wanted to hide and stop the exposure and embarrassment of being helpless and naked in front of him. His upper body was close to hers. His heat radiated the scent of him so alluring, so male. His broad shoulders and gorgeous face, so close, and oh, those succulent lips waiting to be kissed again, and again, and again.

She lay back, sighing and closed her eyes. Luka's warm hand moved up to her belly where he ran it across her flesh. Crisp memories of pleasure with him ignited her, deep below his hand.

"Stop, please," she begged in a whisper. She opened her eyes and looked down to Luka. He smiled his sexy boyish smile, making her spitting mad. He was doing what he did best. This was a deliberate seduction, not inspection.

"I'm glad to see you're mad enough to want me to stop. You're not as injured as I initially feared. But stop? No," he said and shook his head. "I need to see what that bastard has done to every inch of you."

She was confident he wouldn't stop, so instead, she focused on his face where the lines of rage set in, then changed her mind, and pleaded with him.

"Luka, please ... don't ...."

He ignored her.

His icy mood frightened her and the coolness of the air didn't help. It reminded her how naked and helpless she was. To put any weight on her thigh muscles was impossible.

She fought the urge to sit up and pull a blanket over her. Instead, she watched his eyes sparkle, as they wanted each breast. He was weakening, losing the battle with himself. Luka reached out and pulled both of her hands away. Her full breasts flowed to the sides of her chest. Each nipple hardened in response to his hypnotic stare sending a singe to her cheeks. However, she saw his small grin. How it curled about his lips, pleased he had this effect on her.

He touched the gash across one breast, a long red line with flakes of dried blood. He glanced up into her eyes. He burned with the familiar list of grievances against Kaine, and she watched, as it grew longer. His fingertips traced each of her ribs, probing lightly for the extent of her soreness until his hand lay flat on her skin.

Mmmm, the warmth of his hand. It was impossible to stop the pictures of him making love to her, hoping this was the prelude to that incredible act.

He leaned over her. His heaven-kissed long hair, brushed her chest as light as a feather, sending new waves of raised bumps all over her body. Her breaths quickened, and each breath brought pain and pleasure.

"Luka. Please, I ..." She warned as her arms cradled his head.

It was too late. He placed his hot mouth over her nipple and kissed it gently. He ran his lips near the gash, bringing a kiss of comfort to her swollen mound. He raised his head and looked at her.

"That animal will pay for this," he vowed as he brushed a yard's length of her hair back. "I don't understand why he smashed your beautiful face?" He wondered aloud, and the rage flared fiercely in his eyes.

"I don't remember Kaine hitting my face."

"Someone has. You have a bruise and swelling around your eye."

"It wasn't Kaine. I don't remember him hurting me. But then how did all of this happen? It must have been that bitch, Sarah!"

"I'm satisfied you're going to be fine," Luka claimed dismissing her charge against Sarah. He stood, walked over and turned up the thermostat and then hurried into the bathroom and returned as quickly. "The tub is filled. I've added bath salts for healing. Give me your hand."

She looked up at him.

His eyes looked at her, seriously looked at her lying naked. He closed his eyes and exhaled a ragged sigh. He shook his head and raked his fingers through his long hair, trying to rein in his desires.

"Holly if you weren't injured." He stopped and bit his lower lip and glanced away as if to compose his emotions.

He didn't say another word.

She allowed Luka to help her stand. She stood close. Holly took another step closer to him and leaned against his warm body, relieved his arms went around holding her tight. She absorbed his warmth and strength like butter on warm bread.

He pulled her into his embrace and this had nothing to do with steadying her balance. Luka hugged her as if he was relieved no more harm had come to her. He betrayed his motives by naturally slipping his leg between hers. He wanted so much more and Luka held her spellbound.

She buried her face in his strong, sweet-smelling chest. She turned her head a bit to breathe, nuzzling her cheek into him, wrapping her arms around the trunk of his body.

His heart was pounding like a kettle drum, threatening to burst from his chest. He wanted her too, but he was too much of a gentleman. Yet, Luka was so flesh-and-blood. He moved his hands over her tight muscles and they melted her body into a fiery liquid. His warm hand slowly worked its way up each vertebra, with the delicate touch of a butterfly. Inch by fiery inch, Luka massaged her back, up and down, from her shoulders to her thighs until every muscle was relaxed.

Holly snuggled into Luka's healing embrace. And to her surprise, her shattered emotions shot to the surface with a tumultuous speed, making her unable to hold back the tears any longer. They spilled down her cheeks as she cried her pain out on his collar, her cheek nestled against the warmth of his neck. She cried, and she didn't care. Luka was her port in the center of this horrible storm, and she wasn't letting go of him, not until the fear, hate and vengeance in her died a horrible, slow death. She would never let go of Luka. Never. Her emotions had taken an inconceivable beating for the past five days and she was powerless to stop the frustration bottled up a second longer. She continued to explode inside, leaving a shattered heart, a pitiful ruin left by the landfall of the *Hurrikaine*. Huge sobs racked her body, and she collapsed.

Luka caught her in his arms. His embrace pure, warm, and safe.

Her tears of loss, fear, and pain blended, flowing freely.

"Sh ... sh ...! I'm here," he murmured with ease to comfort her. "You've suffered a terrible bloody ordeal. Go ahead and cry," he encouraged, consoling her, stroking her head and when his fingertips moved over her bump, he swore. He kept his hand away from that side of her head after that.

He held her tightly. "I'm here Babe, always close by, always waiting. Cry. Cry that bastard out of your system," he demanded, but his tone was soothing still understanding. His touch was as smooth as raw silk and he was calming her nerves.

Holly listened to Luka's sympathetic words as they reverberated in his chest. His rapid pulse betrayed his calm words. Her sobs became louder as she wrapped her arms further around his waist.

Luka took a step back, pulling his hips away but kept his chest next to her. His hand stroked the line of her face, long and rhythmically, to comfort her. He lifted her chin up to him, bent one finger to wipe away her tears.

She spoke softly. "Why have I been so foolish? You tried to warn me. You were right all along," she affirmed choking on a sob. But she had to ask. "Where were you?"

"Backstage making sure all the video equipment was packed and ready to ship to Paris. Sarah found me and explained Kaine had dragged you away. I was confused that he'd pick Friar Manor to go mental, but I'm not surprised. I was in a panic. Friar Manor's a fucking maze of corridor's, with two never-ending wings. I'll never forgive myself. I knew ... I know Kaine."

"I'll never doubt you again."

"Shhh ... try to put that lout out of your mind. Let's get you into the tub," he replied. He held her a moment longer, offering the security and warmth she desperately needed. Then he gently pressed his lips to her cheek and then brushed her lips with his bringing the familiar sweetness of his closeness.

"There isn't any pain Luka when you kiss me. Your kisses are an elixir for the pain. Kiss me Luka."

"Don't make me say no to you. I'm only human and if I start, I can't promise I would stop."

She saw the self-hatred grow in his eyes because of his limitations.

She stopped caressing his hard chest, the heat of him scorching the palms of her hands.

"No! I'm sorry. I never should have asked you to kiss me. It's selfish of me."

"Let me see your back," Luka suggested, taking a step back, taking a breath, perhaps to ease the sexual tension.

"The surgeon gave me bandages to apply to your ribs, after your bath, if needed. Can you stand on your own?"

"Yes, I believe so."

Luka let go of her saying. "Hold on to my hand."

"I think I should press charges."

"Listen, Babe, I'm going to level with you. Right now, you're the only headline around the world the rags have any interest in publishing. I'm aware you're Holly Hill from the Collins murder trial."

"Does that cause you any problems?"

"Yes. Not personally, but as far as publicity? Think about it. If you press charges, your lawyers are going to win. You should, but what about the members of the band? The hundreds of crew and staff who depend on this tour to feed their families?

It's not between you and Kaine, or you and Sarah. With all the worldwide publicity from the Collins murder trial, the press would love your day in court with Kaine. No, we'll do it my way. I'll find a way to smooth things over with CMT to get you away from Kaine. Don't worry, I have people working on this as we speak."

"You're not saying I have to see Kaine again?" A strong survival urge to run washed over her. She flew into Luka's arms, tightly holding him around the neck, allowing her body to fill the length of him.

His arms pulled her into him with expectations and he released a groan when her hips fit perfectly over his.

He pointed out. "Not if I can stop it. I have favors owed at CMT. I will do what I can to modify your final contest obligations. The last thing you need is to be sued. I'll have my lawyers look into alternative options with Kaine. Never underestimate Kaine or CMT. *Hurrikaine* is a multibillion-dollar corporation. The sponsor and CMT, have a lot of money riding on this tour. The only card we're holding is you counter-suing. It wouldn't go over well if the Duke of Rock 'n' Roll were found guilty of battering his fiancée."

While his words sank in, she had the idea that Kaine did not leave her this way though his reputation preceded him, concerning his violent treatment of previous girlfriends. She wasn't convinced her condition was all his doing. It was then she wondered if she'd experienced a blackout like the doctor described due to the drugs and alcohol and the pivotal events were temporarily lost to her. But if it was Kaine, it meant she didn't want to see him anytime soon.

Confused, she protested. "You can't be serious. Let him

walk?"

Luka was saying something. "Remember how cutthroat the media was with the Collin's murder trial? Well, if they get wind of this, you're going to bloody well be ten times more miserable than you are tonight. You think you're used to managing media decisions, but trust me. Sensational headlines are my business. Let me handle this until you're better. Please, try to relax and trust me. I'm not Kaine."

He threw her a tired smile. "I have to call in a few big favors to keep all the photographs and gossip about Friar Manor out of the papers, remember, you did not leave with Kaine. There will be questions, speculation." Luka reiterated as his smooth hand cupped her chin and gave her an affectionate squeeze.

Holly smiled, trusting him — finally. It had cost her more than she wanted to admit. Luka had been right about Kaine from the start. New tears burst forward uncontrollably, cascading down her cheeks. Tears for Luka, her beautiful angel eyed Luka.

His hand dropped and slid down her body, his mouth opened a bit as if he was debating whether he should follow his instincts and kiss her. His eyes sparkled, worshipping her.

How badly she wished, things were different.

His face grimaced, he'd decided not to kiss her, and he helped her into the water.

She bent slowly until she was submerged.

"You'll be fine for the next half hour. I've calls to make." He insisted abruptly, rushing from the bathroom like a man running from demons.

Holly laid back in the warm, deep, scented water and finally relaxed. She tried to fit the pieces together to figure out how all this happened. The water was cool when Luka returned to rinse her shampooed hair and helped her step out of the tub. Her skin was red and wrinkled. Luka dried her off — every inch, his hands were soft and gentle, hands to nurse and comfort the wounded. Luka became her comforter. Luka finished drying her back and the redness in his eyes returned. He looked away quickly. She caught him using the back of his hand to wipe away his tears.

He was strong and to be caught in this madness, must upset him more than he lets on to her. He was trying to be brave and strong for both of them.

He muttered low, under his breath. "That bastard better not come near me." His eyes said justice was needed, and she agreed. Luka slipped his arm around her waist like so many times before and helped her to bed. He sat her up, fluffing the pillows until they molded to her back, and no matter what he did, every time he touched her she yearned for more of him.

Luka poured water into a glass, showed her where the prescription for the muscle relaxers on the table as a harsh knock came to the door.

There was the room service clerk's muffled word exchange. Luka brought her a large snifter half-filled with a caramel liquid.

"I left the bottle of brandy in the car. Sip this. It will help to soothe your jagged nerves." He prescribed as he sat closer to her on the edge of the bed.

"Soon, I will have a change of clothes delivered. However, for tonight, there's nothing clean for you to wear. You don't need anything tonight."

He half smiled … she half smiled.

If only things were different.

The phone rang and Luka hesitated.

She was sorry for whoever called to disturb him. It might mean their job if it wasn't urgent.

"Hunter! No! Not now!" he yelled. "Can't you bloody well get it through your fucking head? Someone else needs my attention. I'll be there *if*, and when I can. It's probably better I don't see him anytime soon anyway. Handle him. Anyway, you can. Knock him out if you have to. The bastard has it coming," he said and then slammed the phone back on the table.

Luka moved his head to the side raking his fingers through his hair and hung a long lock behind his ear. He stared at her. His icy blue eyes glowed with intensity, asking if she wanted to an update on how Kaine was.

"I don't need any reports," she stated as if disgusted, shaking her head, and trying to roll over to face him.

"I'm bloody well going to fuck him up bad for this."

"Luka, please, no more violence." She wasn't sure Luka had listened. His hands worked her hair free from the entangled towel. Her curls fell all around her shoulders as he leaned in close. She gazed into his beautiful eyes that confessed he loved her too, and when she'd recovered, he was coming after her. She wanted to clutch her breaking heart.

"I'm amazed I made such a horrible mistake. You've been dreading this, hoping to prevent this, knowing it would come. Oh, Luka, how impossible this has been for you."

She saw a sensitive and loving man, a man she'd hurt deeply.

Luka wrinkled his brow and dropped his own bomb. "Tell me why you came to London? Better yet, start with whom you're running from, and why?"

Her lips parted to fall open. Her eyebrows arched pushing wrinkles upon her forehead. "What made you suspicious?" She stammered, not knowing if Brett was important any longer.

"In my line of work, I've learned to read people. And something else going on with you. It doesn't have anything to do with Kaine, or me. Trust me Holly and don't leave anything out."

She didn't argue. The brandy, the shot, soaking in the tub and Luka's magical massage, all blended to afford her the pleasures of warmth and safety if she didn't move. Her comfort zone with him afforded her a loose tongue. For the first time in days, she had a complete sense of well-being with Luka.

She started with Jon, then Brett, the tragic marriage, the attempted suicide. She told Luka how lonely she'd been the past seven years, explained her blood-oath to Brett. She told him about the Collin's trial and her pledge to Brett and the marriage proposal. How she'd only accepted the contest to get away from Brett to give her time to figure out how to reject his idea to set a wedding date without affecting his rising career.

His expression never changed. He sat and listened.

The golden light was cresting the windowsill while the rain fell quietly when she finished the last of her story.

"What have you decided?" he asked calmly, cradling her, his long legs stretched out, crossed at the ankle.

Holly draped half her naked body across his chest. Her bottom half covered with the blanket and Luka hadn't moved.

She was safe, maybe for the first time in her whole life. She slipped her arms up around his shoulders and hugged him. She rubbed her bare breasts against his silk shirt, full of regret because he would not make love to her.

But oh, he felt wonderful — like a beautiful dream.

Chapter Thirteen

BACK TO THE HOUSE THAT LOVE BUILT

The rains continued to fall quietly as if to cleanse her soul. Stripped of all her pride, all the lies, and deceptions, she needed only him.

"Luka...." Holly whispered softly.

She lifted her chin and pressed her lips against his.

He didn't respond.

Please, she begged in her mind.

Holly pressed harder, trying to gain entrance by licking the seam of his luscious lips with her tongue.

Luka wouldn't respond.

She pulled back, disappointment etched on her face.

He spoke after a breath.

"I assume Brett is out of the picture, but that doesn't clear up the other matter. I promised I would wait for you to come to me, to give me your heart. I want you to come to me because you want *me*, not running away from *him*."

He refused to say Kaine's name.

Holly understood.

But she was stubborn and wouldn't listen either as her arm slid over his shirt to where she instinctively pulled each button out of the hole. She wanted her past behind her. She wanted out of Hell. She wanted Luka to take her back to that private place and teach her to fly but wait …. Kaine already taught her to fly.

She stopped.

Kaine took her there.

Fraught with indecision, she remembered the love, the moments when Kaine drove her off the edge to float, to fly.

She fought the destroy guilt that assaulted her and decided to replace Kaine with her sweet Luka.

She placed a moist kiss over his heart. "Let me make it better," she whispered, locking her gaze on his.

His eyes pleaded don't. "You're lost and lonely. You've experienced a terrible shock and I want your head clear of drugs and alcohol, but mostly of Kaine Walker when I touch you. I don't want your anger. I want your love. I want you in love with me."

Holly didn't speak and kissed him again.

"I'm warning you. If you don't stop, I'm selfish enough to take you now." Luka's beautiful angel eyes begged her not to test his words.

She kissed his chest again. "I'll stop if you promise not to leave me," she whispered.

"I'll stay until you're asleep. You will be safe while I'm away. Please, quiet down, let me hold you, comfort you, but please don't ask for more, it will be difficult to say no."

"You asked if I had made a decision. Show me how it will be when we are together. Give me something to dream of,

Luka."

Luka's touch felt soft, balancing the brutality of Kaine.

But there was a missing piece. Why did she want to forget the pain-ridden past, the stifling guilt, and the unbearable betrayal? Where did the guilt and betrayal come from to torment her? Her questions faded as she stared into Luka's half-hooded sexy eyes and watched him fight to control himself. She hoped he'd lose the fight.

He pulled her closer releasing a ragged breath. He moved to adjust himself to lie on his side, wrapping his top leg over hers and cradled her beneath him. He aligned himself with her lips and slanted his head to kiss her — gently at first.

She slid her hands around his warm, strong back and pulled her body against his where she sank into the bliss of Luka's kiss. His fingers traced her jawbone while his lips avoided the swollen side of her lip. She opened her mouth and sucked in his tongue. She kissed Luka a desperate kiss to keep Kaine away. A kiss to forget Kaine as only Luka could.

Luka emptied his soul and devotion into her then broke away.

"Make me forget," she invited in a whisper as she dragged her lips over his cheek to press adjacent to the shell of his ear. She opened her eyes while his lips brushed her neck and wrapped her arm around him.

"Mmmm, you feel wonderful," she admired. Her hand caressed his bronzed chest. "How beautiful you are," she complimented and then smiled.

Luka rolled over on his back gently bringing her with him. When she came to rest on top of him, her long hair became a tent shielding them from the world. Her hand crept up over his shirt to follow the curve of his long, slender neck to his soft, pink kissable lips. Oh, those warm, succulent lips of his that always kissed her to oblivion.

"This isn't the way I envisioned this happening, Babe," he whispered deep and breathy.

"I'm sure you don't, but I need you more than you'll ever believe," she replied.

"I need you too, Babe. But I don't want you to think if I make love to you that it will stop Kaine. He's coming back for you, I can promise you that."

His words stunned her. She'd thought she was finished with Kaine Walker and ping ponging between the headstrong and powerful men.

"Aren't you a bit melodramatic?"

"Have I been wrong yet?"

Holly pretended not to hear him. She didn't want Kaine coming after her. Her fingertips struggle with the next button of his shirt. Her eyes filled with tears again with a new thought arrived. What if Kaine went after Luka to destroy him?

Why would he do that?

There was something about that thought that rang true, but there wasn't a memory to explain why.

"Damn this button." She blurted out from frustration, more over her thoughts than from the annoying button. The cloth ripped while she fumbled. She bent and kissed his beautiful chest. She looked up again as the button popped off his shirt.

"Are you sure you want me since you know he hasn't forgotten you? The son-of-a-bitch is in love with you, you have accepted that, haven't you Babe."

Why did she think this ordeal was over with Kaine? Why

did she believe that he'd turn off his feelings so quickly?

Because she'd tried, to do that — turn off her feelings with Luka.

The unbearable pain was boiling in her heart, cracking, and shattering again. How would she bear it all again? Her beloved ripped from her.

Holly placed her hand over her heart powerless to stop it from breaking. She looked over to Luka and spoke so quietly she watched him strain to listen to her words. "I don't know any more Luka." She leaned back on the pillow to decide if making love with Luka, while she was still so deeply in love with Kaine was fair to anyone, especially Luka.

The cellular phone rang, again, and again.

Luka stopped.

For the first time, it seemed as if, he might refuse to be called away.

She lay quietly.

The phone stopped ringing. He sighed in relief.

She moved closer to him.

But his body was moving away. The phone rang, again, and again. The sharp, annoying sound broke the trance. He would answer this time. No words passed between them.

"Hunter. Fuck! Where's security? There's nothing I can do right now. No, fucking sedate him, I don't care how. And don't let the bloody authorities in there. In fact, do a thorough search of his suite straightaway and get any vials out of there in case they arrive unannounced. No ... soon."

His voice dropped, his eyes shifted avoiding hers. "I'll be there soon."

His words floated over her head with a crestfallen tone.

Luka hung up and leaned back.

"How long?" She didn't want a timetable.

"Until you're asleep."

Kaine needed Luka more than she did. He was going to leave her to go to Kaine. It should be she going to tell Kaine. She felt sorry for something that she'd done that was so horrible it tore him apart — them apart.

Holly needed to remember. This was wrong, all wrong.

Luka finished unbuttoning his blood-splattered shirt and to her surprise took it off and slipping it up each of her arms. The warm shirt engulfed her, soothed her, and carried his wonderful, familiar scent. He buttoned it and rolled the sleeves up until she saw her hands. He leaned his body into her to lean on while she stood. He turned the bedding down for her.

Holly gulped down the last drop of brandy. It wasn't a proper substitute for Luka but was toasty warm and soothing in her belly. She took long, deep breaths to calm her torn and frayed nerves. She didn't miss how smoothly Luka slid under the covers beside her with his trousers and socks on, his subtle dusting of chest hair begging for her touch.

Luka cautiously and gently scooped her up into his arms, and she lay quiet, stroking his chest with long even strokes. His fingers wove in and out of her damp, tangled, hair with long, meaningful strokes and occasionally kissed the top of her head.

The swelling in his Levi's relax, and his breaths even out. It would have been an excellent end to a long night of unimaginable love making if it hadn't been the pathetic scene it truly was.

Luka finally broke the silence. "I'm pleased you wanted to make love to me."

"Since I saw you at the airport."

He didn't answer, but she saw in her mind the smile on his face.

"How long will you be gone?" she finally asked.

"Hours. Security will check on you every hour to check your concussion. They tell me Kaine's done a lot of damage and I have to destroy all media trails. This means more favors. Too much is riding on *Hurrikaine*'s new clean-cut family image. CMT may lose a lot of money and ratings.

"Security's outside, but don't ever answer the door. It may be Kaine. He's tricky and I'm not sure how dangerous he is. What a bloody mess. That reminds me. Don't answer the phone either. It may be Kaine or media. I'll leave my mobile so I can call you. Here is another number I can be reached at if you have any problems. I'm only a call away from you. I'll be back here when I can."

Holly cuddled up close to Luka and molded her body to fill all his curves.

Luka comforted her. "Come on Babe, rest, sleep." While one hand caressed her arm with light butterfly strokes, the other picked up the novel from her bed table she'd brought to read on the airplane.

"I like this author too," Luka revealed with a tired smile.

"Her stories are nothing like the real thing."

Luka flipped to the page Holly had marked and read aloud about vampires posing as rock stars.

Chapter Fourteen

HEAD GAMES

Day 6

The morning's sunlight crept silently over the rooftops of London. The sun rose bright, like a phoenix out of the darkness of the landmark night. The sky burst into a brilliant shade of royal purple, erasing the last of the black shadows, ready for a new day. Black and purple, the *Hurrikaine* logo colors. Would everything remind her of Kaine?

Her dreams were fragments of a dark corridor and seemed all too real. She cautiously sat up, took a sip of an opened mineral water, realizing she couldn't tell where her horrible hangover from all the champagne and cocaine ended and the pain of the ... she couldn't remember.

She looked over at the windowsill and out to the land of Peter Pan. She was no different from Wendy, waiting for her fairy tale man to take her to Neverland. Only then, she realized she wasn't in her suite at the Lainesbough. Why was she here?

She turned to find the bed empty and confirmed that this was her hotel room. She looked down and found that she was wearing a blood-spattered shirt.

Whose blood?

Who's shirt and why?

What happened?

Why was she here?

She moved, but her head was splitting and a jackhammer would have been quieter. She lay back wondering what she should do. She looked over to the bed stand to call, call whom? There she saw a small bottle. It said a medical term for a drug, then read muscle relaxer, take two as needed for pain. Well, she was in pain. She reached for the glass of water and swallowed two and then lay back deciding how hard to breathe because each breath hurt her head.

It was odd to remember Luka, but nothing about Kaine. There were fragments, something about facing a media nightmare. Something about how the Heart of the *Hurrikaine* and her dream man broke off their engagement. She sat up startled and panicked at the realization. The excruciating pain in her head quickly followed and demanded that she stop moving.

What the hell happened?

Too many questions. Why wasn't she by Kaine's side?

She needed answers, but her head hurt, no, throbbed. She decided to go to the bathroom to get a cold cloth, but she found to move a centimeter made her entire body ached as though being put through the first day of boot camp. All her muscles ached, and she discovered quickly where to place any weight on her legs.

What happened?

Her hand traveled the back of her head and discovered a bump the size of a large cherry giving her a moment's worry. She pulled dried bits of blood from her fingertips and inspected it.

What happened?

The absence of collected moments to weave into an explanation terrified her. Something very wrong happened. She needed to remember. She reached for the phone and ordered Lavender Earl Grey tea, biscuits, an empty bag, and ice.

What did Kaine do to her?

"Damn you, Kaine Walker!" She howled like a wolf at the moon while sinking her fist into the pillow. Why did he hurt her so deeply? But she couldn't understand why that didn't sound right. The last thing she'd remembered was talking to Marc LeRouge, and after that, whatever happened to separate her from Kaine came up as a blank, apparently lost to a chemically induced blackout.

Tears dropped from her eyes.

The expected knock came too soon.

She wiped away her tears. The sharp pains lessened thanks to the wonders of the muscle relaxers. But she didn't dare move too fast. She'd either forgotten or subconsciously ignored Luka's warning to answer.

She opened the door.

The security man said in a friendly tone from the other side of the door. "I heard you moving about Miss Hill. Sorry to disturb you. Mr. Hunter insisted on no visitors. But, there's a lady here who's exceedingly persistent, says she knows you and its urgent she speaks with you."

Holly moved to peek out, wondering why Luka decided it

necessary to place security at her door.

Where was he?

Again, what the fuck happened? Her sore legs muscles needed immediate attention, and she surmised a hot bath sounded healing but set out to scoot across the floor, assisted by grabbing on to chairs back and then the wall. She opened the door a bit more and found an attractive, petite lady, dressed in a black *Hurrikaine,* letterman's jacket, black fitted Levi's and boots. Her honey-blond hair hung long and damp. She didn't recognize her, but something about her seemed hauntingly familiar. Her eyes sparkled with a dark, unforgettable blue.

"May I help you?" Holly asked bristling because of the *Hurrikaine* logo.

In a strong, proper British accent, the woman answered with a tiny smile on her lips. "Yes, I'd hope so. I do apologize for the hour, but It's essential I have a word."

Holly remembered Solange's constant warnings about not talking to strangers. So she asked. "You a reporter? Because if you are, I have no comment."

"I'm sorry Holly. How awkward. Of course, you don't remember me. I met you last night at Friar Manor."

Holly understood something happened there that forced her to return to her hotel. She shied away from any confrontations.

"I don't want to talk about Friar Manor. Please!" She moved to close the door.

"I understand your feelings, but it's not that easy. I'm Nicky's wife, Emily. Or, perhaps you might remember me as Kaine's sister?"

Sister?

SUR ... PISE!

"Sister?"

"I understand by your tone and expression no one's told you. May I, please come through?"

"Who you are, doesn't change anything, but yes."

Holly watched the elegant woman walk past her wondering why she'd ask such an odd request to "come through," but then remembered her.

"Yes. You sat at the far end of the table."

How did she miss the same haunting blue eyes?

"I don't usually come calling unannounced or uninvited during the wee morning hours, but these are unusual circumstances. I've left Kaine and I ..."

Not knowing what happened, Holly didn't want to be placed in an uncomfortable position.

"I don't think it's appropriate to speak to you about Kaine Walker."

Another knock on the door interrupted Holly. "Excuse me."

She hobbled toward the door and accepted the tea cart wondering what the hell occurred to leave her wounded and for Kaine to send his sister as an ambassador for his defense.

Holly whirled around and headed slowly toward Emily.

"I can't talk about anything right now."

Suddenly, stinging tears spilled out uncontrollably. Embarrassed, Holly looked over to find Emily sitting quietly, inspecting the bloodstains on the shirt Holly wore.

Yes, Holly wondered too.

Holly placed ice in the bag and applied it to her throbbing and wounded head and then she moved to the table where her medicine sat, including the two vials of cocaine. She turned her back to Emily using her body as a shield and quickly dropped the vials into the pocket of the shirt and then picked up a tissue with her free hand and wiped her eyes.

"You're not well?" Emily asked with sympathetic reserve.

Holly half-smiled sarcastically, glad to have concealed the cocaine and ignoring all the champagne she'd drank. Instead, she admitted. "I have a splitting headache and I'm hoping this ice will bring down the swelling."

"Swelling? What happened?" Emily queried in a cautious tone.

She'd slipped and volunteered too much. Confused by Emily's visit, she ventured, "You said you'd come from Kaine, didn't he tell you?"

"No, he ... couldn't."

Holly's heart leaped. What happened to separate the two of them? Why was he unavailable? Too many questions. Had Luka finally stopped waiting for her and gone after Kaine to silence him?

"Couldn't? Or, wouldn't?" Holly snapped, not wanting to show any concern until she collected more facts, cursing herself for not remembering.

Emily's face told another story.

"Why?" Holly asked with growing concern, but her expression still pretended she didn't care.

"He passed out. My husband, Nicky, and I stopped by his suite because Ian called frantic and upset. We found Sarah there, kneeling beside Kaine on the bed, his suite torn to bits. We didn't know what to think?"

"I'm surprised!"

That was news, and she didn't know what to think either. Holly wondered if he'd scared her, lost his temper again and maybe she shouldn't concern herself any longer with a man who might have literally torn up her life. But pictures of that redheaded bitch irritated her especially hovering around her fiancé, if he was any longer, and they pushed her to ask anyway.

"He's all right?" she asked in an even tone, hoping she didn't give her true intent away.

"Well, he truly gave us a scare. That's why I'm here. I'm keen on finding out what caused Kaine to destroy his suite? It's only because he's Kaine Walker and can pay the damages and more that he wasn't nicked. We couldn't find out why you weren't there with him. Solange suggested we try to look here for you. The concierge wouldn't confirm your presence so I came here on my own. Did the pairs of you have a terrible row?"

"Oh yes," she confirmed nodding her head deciphering "row" must mean fight. "We must have had a terrible row. Come here and touch our row."

Emily's facial expression filled with hesitant curiosity. She walked over to Holly and placed her fingertips on Holly's swollen knot.

"No! Please tell me Kaine didn't do this?"

Emily's beautiful blue eyes darkened with fear.

"This relationship has moved much faster than I anticipated. I do need to talk with you."

"Well, as much as I appreciate your concern, I feel like shit, my head won't stop throbbing, and last night ... well, you need to get the details from Kaine. Please ... I would like to rest. This has been the longest damn week of my life," she conceded, hoping she'd covered her trail, trying to beg off since the past eight hours were lost to the blackout.

"I can understand how overwhelming the whole *Hurrikaine* experience has been. I'm not convinced you should be alone for many reasons. I would prefer to stay, keep you company ... chat."

There was no getting around the determined woman.

Emily was staying.

"You do?"

Assuming Kaine, lost his temper again and scared her, she said.

"Well, let me tell you what your brother did to me last night."

Holly filled in the few details she remembered since Emily wanted details. It was then she realized there were vast gaping holes of missing time. How was she going to blast Emily with the unvarnished truth about Mr. Walker?

Between tears, Holly unfolded as much of the story as she remembered after Kaine sang the solo. She thought it wise to leave out the proposal and marriage plans because perhaps they'd been canceled.

She moved on with her story, starting with when she'd entered the ballroom.

The problem, there wasn't much to tell. She couldn't remember anything after meeting Marc LeRouge. If her body hadn't been bruised and sore, or awakened alone in her suite, she wouldn't have known anything bad happened to her the previous night. Then, like Emily, she would have wondered why she wasn't with Kaine too.

Emily's warm heart and compassionate suited Holly as she listened, but the confusion on her face questioned, what happened? Holly hoped her confession would send Emily away.

But she couldn't find any reasons to be away from her beloved. Instead, she found herself crying into Emily's arms because the pain in her heart became unbearable.

Emily stroked Holly's hair lightly and then rested her hand over the large lump saying. "Well, this bump tells us something has happened to you. Let's hope this wasn't part of what transpired between you and my brother. Here, allow me to get soap and water to clean your wound."

Emily returned and carefully parted Holly's hair.

"Don't worry. It's a tiny gash, but head wounds can be bloody."

Holly started to breathe a little easier and relaxed.

Emily delicately cleaned the wound and continued, "I was told that after leaving the manor, Kaine continued to drink himself into a stupor and passed out. But not before a hideous display of self-contempt. I'm not sure what mood he will be in when he wakes, or what he will remember, but I thought there are a few things you should be made aware of ... before you see my brother again."

Holly's beaten physical condition was evidence enough that something intolerable happened between them.

One thing was sure.

"I'm never, ever, seeing Kaine again!" Holly exclaimed adamantly.

"You will. My big brother has fallen deeply in love with you and he will come to you."

Chapter Fifteen

STAND BACK

Emily captured Holly's full attention. Holly slowly moved to the settee.

He's fallen deeply in love with you.

But she already believed that and so much more. Perhaps she wasn't up for Kaine's kind of love.

Holly's well-chosen words tumbled out seeming like an automatic response.

"Emily, you've cleaned my wound. I'm not sure I can survive his kind of love."

"Maybe if you understood what it is to be Kaine ... and then to be Kaine in love, you could find it in your heart to forgive him? You be the judge. I'm not sure of how much history you have on Kaine?"

"Not much from him."

"Well, with Kaine, all of his feelings are intense. He can be so stubborn and single-minded, which is what you fell in love with. I can imagine how overwhelming and wonderful that must have been, especially when you were the focus of his unending love pouring out on you."

Holly shook her head comfortably, in agreement. Nothing prepared her for Kaine in love.

"He is an exceedingly special and complicated man. You're indeed lucky to have him in love with you."

"Lucky?" she blurted out.

Lucky to escape, she thought.

The strong reaction twisted her waist causing her to wince with pain, reminding her need for a hot, healing bath. Instead, she cautiously moved off the settee.

Holly poured a cup of tea into the supplied bone china cup, offered a cup to Emily, and then poured a second.

"Let me do something to help." Emily picked up a brush and parted Holly's matted hair into sections. She carefully brushed out Holly's long strands. Emily started to unfold her narrative of her brother, a man named Kaine.

"Kaine's mother, an American like you, was killed in an auto accident when he was fifteen. He was brought here to live with a man he never knew existed, our father, Edward Dunnehill. Without drawing too bleak a picture, Kaine mourned heavily over his mum's unexpected death, and father lived an entirely different lifestyle. Father made Kaine feel like an outsider as if he could never measure up to his standards. It was no secret Father wanted a male heir and poor mother was barely able to carry me to term. Father expected a lot of the son he never knew."

Holly squirmed, sipping her tea, not sure, she wanted sympathetic feelings for Kaine, but his devoted advocate continued.

"Kaine was brash, wild and never fit in at social gatherings that were Father's only pastime. Father was what's known as an

English gentleman, which means nothing except he didn't formally earn a living. Father inherited a lot of old family money and believed he was a true aristocrat. He loved his Cleveland Bays and playing polo, a nine-goal player he was. What was interesting, Kaine had been raised with horses, rode what he called the rodeo circuit, so that became their only bond, horses.

"Mother and Father traveled much of my childhood, leaving me to be raised by a string of governesses until Kaine arrived. He became the first stable person in my life, an ally, and smashing new friend, and my brother.

"Kaine was brilliant, and different from the start because he was raised in a simpler life, a trailer in the Arizona desert, free to ride his wild horses and sing songs with his mother. He told such thrilling stories.

"He wasn't impressed with Fathers' stables, the estate, or fathers' aristocratic crowd. The only thing that warranted his attention was the castle. Kaine loved to hide out in the castle."

"Castle?" Holly choked, almost afraid to ask *which* castle.

"Why yes. I see, it's like him to stay private. He hasn't told you yet, the video shoot at the castle, that's his home. Briarwood Estate belongs to Kaine. I live in Briarwood Cottage by the lake."

Emily seemed surprised that Kaine chose not to tell her that Briarwood belonged to him.

Holly realized she'd never thought to ask Kaine where he lived. It never came up in conversation. It was then she heard his words.

Briarwood is as far as the eye can see.
If you were Mistress of Briarwood.

And oh, how she'd gone on and on criticizing the owner. No wonder he didn't mention it then. But something inside her said she'd known all along, the way he shared details about the castle. She'd been afraid to believe the fantasy could be that real, Kaine could be a fairy tale come true!

It was difficult to remember all the conversations with Kaine when she'd labeled the owner as cold and selfish. How horrid she'd been. The all too familiar flush to her cheeks arrived and stung with embarrassment, which turned like quicksilver to anger. She wondered why Kaine had been so insulting.

Was he testing her?

Why hide the truth from her?

He hadn't trusted her after all.

Emily sipped her tea and continued brushing Holly's hair.

"Solange shared bits of your castle adventures with me. I do hope you don't mind. She thinks you're so good for my brother. I'm pleased he trusted you enough to take you to his secluded refuge. No one's allowed there except family … the band."

Interesting. He'd taken her home to his private world.

Emily, like her brother, spun a magic spell around her, so magical that her anger started to dissolve.

"Dunnehill Manor was where we lived with Father and Mother. Life there was a horrible nightmare from which we couldn't wake up."

"I've experienced a little of that life." Holly reluctantly admitted trying to ease Emily's quivering voice and noticed Emily's hand trembled as she brushed the lock of her hair.

"Father was terribly controlling and horribly abusive."

The lashes, Kaine's father, beat him mercilessly. She'd bet

anything.

Holly smiled, glad Emily stopped by to visit. She was still angry with Kaine, but now she had insight into his mercurial moods and good to have a few questions answered. At least, understand why she would never see Kaine again.

"Kaine held on to the estate for me, my childhood home, but he grew to love the castle," Emily explained as she finished Holly's hair and sipped more tea.

Holly stood to stretch her sore muscles and instantly regretted it.

"I'll order more tea."

Emily agreed and continued. "After a while, trouble brewed over Kaine's incessant infatuation with pubs, his love for playing guitar and singing torch songs like his mother. Anne was her name."

Holly interrupted, "Interesting, he did tell me that. Coincidentally, my middle name and my mother's name is Ann."

Emily smiled at the twist of fate. "His mum sang in the local Country-Western bars as Kaine called them and waitressed during the day. They were very, very close. I envied his warm-hearted stories about her. She sounded lovely, and he loved her so. That's the muse of Kaine's powerful ballads, much like the one he has written for you."

Holly recalled how Kaine touched on this story and then dared to ask.

"Tell me about Edward Walker."

"Oh, Fathers' name was Dunnehill, Edward Dunnehill. Father was the complete opposite of Anne and Kaine. Father was a wicked and brutal man, tall as Kaine, equally handsome, could charm the wings off a fly though he'd rather pull them off. He had a vile temper, although he never let anyone but Mother, Kaine, and I experience it. A good part of Fathers' brutality fell on Kainc when he came home from the pub. He would beat him with anything around, but his favorite was the riding crop. A few times, it was so bad that he tore Kaine's backup, and all I could do was sneak into Kaine's room and care for him. Father was exceedingly cruel. He'd lock Kaine up for weeks on end not wanting the world to see his handiwork. It was as if Father thought he could beat the love of music out of Kaine."

Riding crop, lash marks on his back.

How ghastly. Nevertheless, there was the confirmation, quieting her suspicions. She'd wanted to believe the lashes were caused by something else, but as at the castle, her intuition was spot on and thriving.

That released horrifying thoughts to circle her thinking. It was his father that torn up his back. Her sore muscles reminded her how much he must have ached from his father's torture and tried to understand Kaine's suffering.

"But Kaine loved his music more than the routine beatings. Nothing, even Father, could stop Kaine. Eventually, Kaine didn't come home much. He hid out in the castle. Father disliked Kaine hanging around with musicians and artists. Father saw Kaine's behavior as bringing disrespect on the family and it had been bad enough without a male heir. But this was a public insult, Kaine parading about with his nefarious ways."

"Was the public insult, is it a British attitude or parental?"

"The problem was both. I can see you need the complete story to understand. Briefly, my father was Edward Dunnehill the third, Duke of Dunnehill. Kaine changed the name of the estate to Briarwood, a favorite childhood name of mine, as a present for my eighteenth birthday. It was Fathers' attitude that no one should ever bring shame on the family name. I don't know how much you understand about the royal peerage, but Kaine's inherited the title of Duke, the only title that can be inherited that is not of royal nobility. Grandfather was a first cousin to the Prince."

Holly was impressed now. Kaine, a Duke. An aristocrat. She could see a bit of it when he stood straight and carried his head high.

The tea arrived and Holly assured as she poured.

"I couldn't be more surprised. Kaine, he's *the* royal rock star?"

Holly spoke too abruptly, embarrassed by her outspoken response. She'd remembered yesterday's headline and reported.

"Duke of Rock finds Duchess. I thought it was a catchy title. But Kaine's a real, honest-to-goodness duke?"

"Afraid so, it's him. The papers chronicled his disgrace and especially the dirty details for a long time — mostly, about turning his back on duty for music."

Holly shrugged her shoulders. She didn't know what she thought anymore. She'd a faint recollection of headlines a decade ago about a musician and royalty. Then she remembered the lowly title she'd christened him in the castle's kitchen, Sir Lancelot de *Hurrikaine*. All the times she and the crew called him Lord, or, Your Grace, at the video shoot, she'd thought it was part of the act, the enchantment of the castle, the game. Not so. Everyone was showing Kaine, a royal duke, his or her respect.

That's why. She suddenly realized, understanding his secrecy and protecting himself.

Emily was talking as she walked.

"It's all perception. You can see straightaway the problems with becoming a Duke. Kaine treated everything Father held in high regard with succinct hatred. Worse, Kaine couldn't have cared less he was of royal lineage. He saw himself as an American. To add further insult, Kaine wouldn't carry Fathers' sir name."

"Quite a rebel, isn't he?" Holly applauded, with surprising pride as she leaned back wincing in pain.

Kaine had been a strong man to stand up to his cruel father. But apparently, she'd seen him acting like Edward Dunnehill a few hours ago.

Yes, Kaine was a complicated man, and tiny twinges fluttered in her heart. Was it softening?

"I was sixteen when our parents were killed, the international press and Fleet Street came down heavy, and my aristocratic relatives would have nothing to do with me. Therefore, I lived with Kaine, and then only eighteen, he became my legal guardian.

"But the surprise — father spent nearly all the family fortune and there wasn't much to inherit, except Dunnehill Estate, which is enormous. Kaine didn't want the land, but I did. It was lean times, but he kept the estate for me and continued to raise the Cleveland Bays, as Father had, to pay the taxes. We even had to turn his private refuge, Dunnehill Castle, into a museum, a tourist attraction, to make extra money to survive. He was bitter, and that's why no one is ever allowed in the castle."

"That explains why Kaine didn't finish restoring it. He didn't want people in there?"

"Correct," Emily stated.

Holly yawned, more as a signal she had finally relaxed with Emily's companionable visit, then fading fast. Yet, there had been too many days in the eye of the *Hurrikaine*. Everything started to blur. She'd been up too long. And if she was going to listen to Emily finish her story she needed more tea.

Her body ached more than she wanted to let on, and excused herself, to shuffle off to wash her face with cold water. Gazing into the mirror, her reflection presented a face that was drawn and tired. Her eyes were red and puffy from crying. A light bruise settled around the top eyelid. Her top lip on the same side was swollen but didn't hurt.

She shook her head.

She was a fucking mess, and she had Kaine Walker to thank for that.

Holly spotted the pile of torn cloth and bloody remnants resting on the floor. She wondered why she wore this blood-spattered shirt and if it belonged to Luka. He'd apparently been there last night since he'd placed security at the door. Perhaps, he was the last person she'd seen before passing out and had all the dirty details that eluded her.

She offered Emily more tea and sat down on the couch with a bit of an attitude adjustment because the muscle relaxers and caffeine were affording her a slight boost and braided her hair into one long plait down the front.

Emily sat on the settee, crossed her legs in a yoga posture, and continued.

"It's been a hard life. In the bands early days, there were

records that hit the charts and the money trickled in but so did the drugs. And, believe me, Holly, we lived the consummate rock musician's life. Why we single-handedly invented new legends. "

She grinned at her exaggeration. "A few stories ... anyway. When the drugs took over, we were isolated, traveling all the time and staying high, myself included. Everything ended in violence." Emily explained with a sad tone.

"We feared Kaine would do away with himself? Sometimes his depression was so bad, well. He was doing heavy drugs. He'd fight with anyone around and broke things. Understand, I'm leaving out significant chunks of time because of the hour."

Holly glanced up to see the sunlight breaking out for a moment, but as quickly a new assault of thick, gray rain clouds smothered the light.

She understood Kaine's depression, what it was like to want to die, and couldn't.

"Kaine got clean and sober. In fact, the whole band did, including me. Kaine found a degree of peace and fulfillment in his music, the ultimate joy in his life ... until you. I see he is lucky to have you in love with him because if you weren't Holly, you wouldn't have been willing to listen.

"The problems we found this morning — all the danger signs are back. It seems Kaine's violent. He's drunk. I'm told he does cocaine, and I saw his suite, he's destroying things again. Something's torturing him. And while I wouldn't presume to advise you, he is worth loving. No one will ever love you as he does.

"However, you should also be warned, his is a harsh lifestyle, I know firsthand. If you're not strong enough ... it will crush you. I hope this visit will help you decide what to do today so the pair of you can work out your differences. Because Kaine does love you and will come for you."

Holly remembered the castle. She remembered Kaine saying.

I hope you can take the lifestyle. I hope you love me enough, through the fucked times.

Well, this certainly qualified as another *fucked* time and they were happening more frequently.

Holly knew she loved Kaine, but was it enough to survive in his 'take no prisoners' world?

Chapter Sixteen

HOLD ON TO MY HEART

K*aine will come for you.*
A brisk knock on the door startled both of them.
"Kaine," Holly blurted.

A rush of adrenaline flashed within her body. She hesitated and looked to Emily, who wore the same look of apprehension. Neither was ready for a confrontation with Kaine.

"Wait, a minute." Holly insisted, stalling, wondering where security was. She hobbled to the door and once again, her body reminded her that it was still painful and difficult to shake how engrossed she'd been with Emily's riveting tale.

"Who's there?"

A familiar voice responded, "Babe? It's me. I hear voices. Are you okay?"

Relieved the predicted confrontation with Kaine was postponed, but surprised that Luka was there, she joyfully opened the door.

Luka swooped in holding a large bag and gently slipped his arms around Holly's waist. He smoothly pulled her into his rugged leather jacket. He lifted the blue, silk shirt up a bit too much, exposing to Emily, the mere fact that Holly wore nothing beneath the shirt.

"I couldn't leave sooner, Kaine's such a mess. I had to hire a bloody cleanup crew for the suite to avoid any repercussions with the hotel or authorities."

Before she reacted, Luka had placed his smooth cheek next to hers. He affectionately hugged her as his fresh scent engulfed her. He lifted her inches off the floor, enthusiastically. The motion caused more pain to her sore muscles than she wanted to admit. Before she cried out, he'd set her down on the carpet and his succulent lips covered hers while his tongue entered her mouth quickly. He kissed her deeply, exploding with his one of a kind passion, leaving tiny sounds of pleasure lodged in his throat. He dropped the bag and his hand drifted down, slowly from her chin to where he cupped her bare cheek and held on tight like a frequent lover.

Luka pulled her closer, to ride on his thigh.

"Mmmm, Babe." He evoked with a lusty breath, between kisses down her neck.

"I've missed you. I brought a change of clothes, toiletries, and fresh bandages along with one of my shirts. We can throw this one away, I won't be needing it."

As usual, the sting of embarrassment burned in Holly's cheeks. What happened that Luka was acting as her protector, her lover? She needed details, quickly, and she hoped Luka had them. But for now, she was sure that Emily would certainly jump to the wrong conclusions as she was. She needed to tell Luka they were not alone before he touched her in places that Emily shouldn't see to report.

"What? You're different?" He stiffened and his eyes

narrowed as if his keen senses told him something was wrong.

Holly stepped back into his arms, pushed up her eyebrows, and shifted her glance to the far corner of the room as she quickly pulled the shirt down and then pointed out.

"Emily's here with me."

Luka spun around wearing a scowl on his face. His unfriendly reaction surprised Holly. She took a step behind him.

"Emmy? Looking out for big brother?" He chided with a cold, sarcastic edge.

Emily ignored Luka's remark and looked to Holly.

It wasn't possible to miss the decided chill between these two.

"It's been an exhausting night and morning. It's time I left and let you have a lie-down, Holly," Emily retorted stiffly, eyeing Luka with blatant contempt. She bent and gathered her belongings. Then she moved past Luka, who towered over her. She approached Holly and leaned in close to say. "Remember what I've told you, hold on, you can, and will, work it out. My brother loves you."

Before Emily left the doorway, Luka slipped his hand under the shirt Holly wore and possessively roamed her derrière. Emily closed the door behind her, but not before, she glanced back over her shoulder. Her lovely face was worn and tired, but her eyes were filled with disgust and disappointment.

Yes, it's true.

Luka was a problem.

What was she going to do about him?

Luka let her go, took off his jacket, and it landed on the floor with a thud.

"I'm acting like a lad in school. I couldn't wait to get back to you." Luka confessed as Emily closed the door, pulling the back of Holly along the length of his body.

"What did she want?"

"Concerned about Kaine."

"She's upset you?"

"No."

Luka turned her around and gently held her.

"Please, explain what has happened that I am here without Kaine?"

Luka was apparently taken aback.

"Babe, what do you mean?"

"Exactly what I said. What happened to me last night that I would wake up here alone?"

"Well, I couldn't be more surprised. But considering all you drank and well the cocaine ... what do you last remember?"

Holly got him up to speed with Marc LeRouge, her last clear memory.

Luka wore the expression of, so you don't remember.

"I'm not sure I should be the one to tell you."

"Tell me what you know," she demanded.

Luka took her hand and led her over to the bed and sat down bringing her beside him.

"You win, I'll tell you what I know."

He spun a fantastic story about her socializing at the party: the kiss, Kaine's reaction, the corridor at Friar Manor, the doctor, and her insistence that she was not going back to Kaine.

Holly was crestfallen and his recollections left her heart shattered.

She'd lost the Precious One.

She'd betrayed him, with — Luka.

"So how did it go at the penthouse?" she asked as she lightly pressed her hand against his chest to brace herself. The story had been worse that any horrible nightmare.

But Luka sat quietly, allowing his tale of betrayal and revenge to settle in deep. He'd showered, shaved, and changed his clothes. The light blue flannel shirt smelled clean and fresh, soft to touch and inviting. She leaned forward and rested her head on his broad chest.

"That's better Babe. Let me hold you. And if you want to know how it went, I'll tell you."

"I'm not sure anymore. Tell me, if it upsets me more, I'll let you know."

"When I went to Kaine's suite, I found Emily hovering over a pissed Kaine."

"Pissed? He's still mad?" She interrupted.

"No! Drunk, it's what we call it. I overheard Emmy ask Solange where you might be staying since no one knew why you weren't there and I didn't offer. I knew something was up and considering how Emily has gone mental on Kaine's girlfriends in the past, I thought I should get here straightaway to run interference and head off the inquisition. The last thing you needed was Kaine's family on your back. Did she come down hard?"

"No. In fact, she is a sweet and kind lady. She believes Kaine is in love with me and is rooting for reconciliation."

Holly leaned back and looked at him realizing two things. One, he'd known Emily was there, and he purposely marked his territory with her, and two, everyone believed she and Kaine only had a lover's argument and that she was still Kaine's girlfriend. She wondered what Luka thought about that, but knowing him, not much, he didn't care when it was true.

She attempted to relax in his embrace, but she needed to understand what happened at Friar Manor. The events were unimaginable. Kaine broke their engagement because she'd betrayed him with Luka. How many words of hate and pain had Kaine shared with her, to describe his heart broken, his dreams shattered? The disgust and shame were too much to bear on top of her bleeding and broken heart.

Luka backed off and looked down into her eyes, lovingly, gently.

"I wanted to make sure you were okay. Listen, since you don't seem to remember to take care of yourself, I've made reservations at a casual restaurant. It will be smashing to get out your last night in London. If you want to order proper clothes, take this."

He handed her English notes folded in a money clip.

"I didn't think you would want to dress posh. There's enough for the basics. If not, use this number. I have an assistant waiting for you to ring, she'll bring over any items that you might need."

"You think of everything."

Now that she knew the ugly truth, she knew better than to argue with him about the cash because he wasn't leaving a credit card paper trail for when it got out she wasn't with Kaine.

"I have more business to do. I stopped a photo of me carrying you out to the car at Friar Manor. Those fuckers were everywhere. There is more work to do. I have to minimize the break-up because tomorrow morning it will hit the front page of every rag across Europe."

"Luka ... is Kaine okay?" She hated herself for asking.

"Don't you worry your pretty head about that lout. He's someone to stay away from, Babe. He has a big problem that goes way back, having nothing to do with you."

"The drugs?"

"That and other things."

He leaned in and swiftly kissed her cheek.

She wanted Luka's affection and here he was about to leave her again. She wanted to sink into his strong, capable arms and have his incredible hands stroke her body until she purred with desire. She looked up at him. She thought how awful she was leading Luka on last night and because of her selfishness and insensitivity, she'd lost Kaine because he'd saw her betrayal. A fitting end to her fractured fairy tale.

His voice was smooth and breathy.

"Don't, Babe. Don't look at me with those eyes."

"What eyes? Eyes that say you need to go away and never come back!"

And what she didn't say was, she was thankful he'd taken care of her and protected her and proved that he did love her too.

Instead, she pressed her body into his, as her arms slid up his chest to rest her hands on those broad shoulders. She curled her hands around the locks of damp hair clumped about his neck. Luka smelled incredibly masculine as she pulled his head down until her lips were even with him. She took a deep breath and wet her lips.

"Don't do this," he pleaded as her lips brushed his.

"We need to say goodbye, Luka."

Luka was quick with his torment, kissed her briefly with restraint, and then leaned away leaving her wanting more.

"I'll come 'round, in the late afternoon and we'll pop out for dinner straightaway and relax. Lock the door and get some bloody sleep. I'll tell security no visitors and I mean none. I'm not saying goodbye, I'll be back for you."

Holly barely smiled, disappointed with her indecent behavior, and slipped out of his embrace. Her only consolation, Luka wasn't smiling either as he closed the door behind him.

She ordered English tea, biscuits, jam, beer to chill, and all the English newspapers available. She settled in to figure out what happened, where it left her, and what she might face today. It was clear, her love affair with Kaine was finished.

It was time to move away from Luka. Not because she'd shared a betraying moment with him, but because she did love him in a mysterious way. However, that strange love wasn't anything like her forever love for Kaine. She must be very careful not to encourage Luka, she would go home and put London far behind her.

Chapter Seventeen

ALONE AGAIN, OR

Time passed slowly. Holly had changed into Luka's clean shirt before the serving cart arrived.

A box sat on top, a long, silver box, with a three-inch red, satin ribbon tied around it.

Holly poured tea, added cream, and sugar, a trick she'd learned from Kaine, and then spread apricot jam on her biscuits. Each a difficult task, because the box, demanded to be opened.

She knew who it was from.

He'd found her.

She was too much of a coward to read his words of goodbye, apparently, he'd needed to say them again. But she'd decided that he represented her past, and even though she was devastated, she had to get ready to go back to L.A., the real world.

Kaine, her Precious One. Her head fell into her hands. Her thoughts were obsessive, thinking only of him. How did he survive in such a crazy world? How lost and lonely, Kaine must be.

As she sipped on her tea, she opened the newspaper, to see a front-page picture with a giant caption:

WHO HAS THE HEART OF THE HURRIKAINE?

A pictorial ran beneath it. One picture of Kaine singing "My Lady," at Friar Manor, another picture showed their silhouette kissing in front of the palace. Another particularly disgusting picture of Kaine with Sarah hanging on him identified her as *his longtime personal assistant.*

This fiasco was also, what Kaine had awoken to, and she thought about how much he must hate her.

And Luka, media savvy Luka, couldn't save the day, there she was. Her life splashed on the cover to read about over morning tea. These pictures were a devastating blow, hitting the bullseye in her stomach, forcing her to sit on the settee.

She grabbed another paper and read.

THE HEART OF THE HURRIKAINE EXPOSED

As she read on, it listed her statistics: name, occupation, and origin. It mentioned her long affiliation with the Collin's murder trial. She was no longer a secret. The article contained a brief history of the Hard Rock video shoot, Briarwood Castle, and a short conjecture on their whirlwind relationship. And, of course, the speculation — would she become the Duchess of Briarwood.

Amazing.

Holly Hill ascribed an English title, and the thought astounded her. Kaine knew all along what her relationship with him meant. He'd kept saying it, trying to protect her. The silver lining — no one reported whatever happened between them at Friar Manor —.yet!

Holly opened the paper to find more photos. The mystery woman at Sir William's benefits bash. And because Kaine was part of the royal peerage, she understood why he captured the interest of the newspapers and tabloids. And why she'd become the focus of fairy tales and dreams, the commoner to marry a royal.

Why hadn't Kaine chosen to tell her any of this?

Amazing, and damn him.

He'd left her unprepared.

There were many photos of her. One looked as if John Roberts held her a bit suggestively when he innocently leaned over to whisper in her ear.

But that's not how it appeared.

There were other equally condemning pictures, with other rock stars, she simply didn't remember. The psychopathic paparazzi knew exactly how to catch the light, their expressions or jesters to present their warped interpretations.

But the photo that put her head on the chopping block and the hatchet in Kaine's hands was the photo of her with, Luka. It forced the cry of damnation from her throat and the punch to her stomach — guilty —.as charged

Tears exploded, dripping from her eyes until the heaving sobs grew loud and then louder.

That fucking photographer — the bastard caught her in Luka's arms with her body coiled around him, his hands cupping her buttocks.

And what a sexy kiss it was.

That's what caused Kaine to call the engagement off, and she couldn't blame him.

How could she?

And that was when she remembered — everything.

You looked like you were fucking him.

Kaine screamed, the disgust and betrayal so vivid in his eyes and he was right.

She shook her head.

She screamed out releasing her pain in the room. Her heart sank, broken in half, and she fell to the floor, taking the paper with her. She sat reeling back and forth on her haunches as the sobbing grew heavier.

That's when the horrific pictures of the corridor focused in her mind. It was all true. It had been her. She had been the one to cause all this pain and confusion. The worry and concern over her betraying actions were destroying Kaine, affecting Kaine's friends, family, and even Luka.

Everything was because of her.

She remembered Luka's passionate kiss and the pleasure, seconds later the lashing humiliation harked its return. She'd figure out the reasons for Kaine's anger.

To continue her moment of self-chastising, she decided neither Kaine nor Luka, deserved her because she hadn't brought either happiness. And Sarah may be right, she ought to crawl off and never come back.

"Fucking great," she said crumpling the newspaper, discarding it in the trash can beside her on the floor.

What will Kaine say when he sees these?

"These photos will surely vindicate his belief that, I'm Luka's ...," she couldn't bring herself to repeat the words out loud or the degrading term he'd called her, without the burn of truth.

In fact, the filthy photos were the evidence Kaine needed to prove her that exact thing.

It was then she remembered how Solange and Kaine warned her of the reporters and how she would be easy pickings.

Solange had been correct.

The Collins murder trial had been no match for the media circus that hounded *Hurrikaine*. They'd all been exactly right.

She'd never known what she was up against — she'd never had a chance.

Kaine, he'd known.

Holly sat holding her stomach, convinced it was possible for her to empty it if it wasn't already. The sense of despair gutted her as she slowly stood and walked over to gaze out the window at the charming street.

It was time.

She needed to face her accuser.

Chastising herself for acting like the coward she was, she accepted a shot of courage and forced herself to walk over to the silver box begging to be opened. Between sobs, she summoned courage. She deserved his condemnation. She lifted the lid of the box before reading the card.

There lay a single red rose, soft as velvet and romantically fragrant. Holly picked the rose up to inhale its scent, a scent so thick, she could practically taste it.

Like Kaine, it was beautiful and pleasing to her senses.

She hesitated before opening the attached card, then flicked the flap and withdrew the card from the tiny envelope.

She took a deep breath, then exhaled, and read on in shock.

My Lady Love....
Forgive me. Here's my heart.
Love me, marry me, but please don't leave me.
I love you so much.
Yours always, Lance.

Kaine's tender words slapped her with an overwhelming guilt. He still loved her. These words were not what she expected. Perhaps he would send a firm goodbye, if anything, but not his pleas for forgiveness and surely not to continue with their plans in Paris.

Holly held the fragrant rose close to her heart. Her body and soul missed him. But she wondered if he would still want her after he saw the morning papers.

But it was his comfort she sought, his kiss, and gentle caress. She wanted to do the same for him, to ease and erase the pain and feelings of betrayal she'd caused him.

They needed each other.

For a moment, she almost smelled him, felt his touch, and him deep inside her.

The tears flowed down again over her cheeks like an unending waterfall. She grasped at the center of her chest, would this aching pain in her heart ever stop? How could she stay away from her magnificent Kaine?

She recognized that she loved him deeply — but she also feared him — he'd hurt her — or — had he?

There were still questions, and the answers apparently locked in a mist she couldn't quite see.

Chapter Eighteen

ALMOST HEAR YOU SIGH

Holly awoke with a start. She sat up to discover her body twisted in the dress shirt wet with her sweat. "Damn! A wonderful dream," she moaned aloud.

A beautiful dream she couldn't shake. She plopped backward to snuggle under the covers and struggled to continue the dream.

Like many vivid dreams, she could feel Kaine wrapped around her and the scent of him strong. It was as if he'd come to her as a dream lover, slipped into her bed when she was the most vulnerable and then melted into her dream and loved her.

Holly missed Kaine desperately.

Time wasn't making it any easier. She glanced at the clock. She'd barely slept a few hours, but there was a slight improvement. She stood. Her body still ached as if physically stretched beyond her capabilities during an extreme workout. She stifled a sarcastic laugh, some improvement. She soaked in a hot tub, washed her hair, and eventually climbed out to dry.

She was thankful her head no longer pounded. She took half a muscle relaxer and decided to go out for a short, slow walk.

After all, it was her last day in London, and there were places she'd dreamed of visiting and necessary to buy something new to wear for dinner that night with Luka.

Luka ... she shook her head. What was she going to do about him? To think about her betrayal with him set her blood to boil. He'd known what he was doing — engineering the end of Kaine.

All of Holly's clothes and personal items were at Kaine's penthouse, so she looked in the bag Luka brought. There she found a clean blue and white, flannel shirt, a brown pair of his trousers that were excessively long, amber colored cashmere socks, and slippers. She dropped the towel, dressed, and tucked in the fresh shirt.

Well, the outfit was ridiculous. Apparently, he didn't want her to leave the suite. She planned to disregard his instructions and go out. It was imperative that her first stop be for new clothes.

Holly pulled a comb gingerly down a long lock of her freshly shampooed hair, careful to avoid her injury. She washed her face carefully and since her make-up bag was at Kaine's, she was through primping.

After filling her nose, with one half-full vial of cocaine, she hoped for a jet-propelled boost for her excursion and then dropped the other vial into her pocket. For now, she was thankful Luka brought this perk into her life.

Security escorted her downstairs under the pretense to pick up her credit cards and passport locked away in the hotel safe. Then she asked the guard to go for a *Daily Sun* newspaper and to slip it under her door. While he was away, she ducked out the side entrance of the lobby, using Kaine's old trick, avoiding the abrasive press and hailed a Hackney cab a block away, another trick.

Following a quick, satisfied smile she instructed, "Kings Road."

Free for the first time Holly strolled along the street. Chelsea was beautiful. It was cool and the brisk air blended with her buzz to revive her, putting a spring in her step. She stopped at a boutique and put on a long-sleeved, fitted, dark-olive, cotton-tweed blend three–quarter length dress, with a low-scooped neck. Around her neckline, she draped a long black and cappuccino-colored, alpaca scarf. She also selected a beautifully tailored, black, wool jacket and mini skirt suit. She carefully chose a pair of black leather, knee-high boots, and a large, walnut-colored, leather bag.

Holly threw in black silk lingerie, no longer caring if Luka would appreciate them. She passed a store window and noticed her reflection dressed in the new, fashion-forward clothes, compared to the conservative white suit she'd worn the first day. The thought brought a gratified smile at how much she had transformed in six short days.

Holly took on a slower gait aware the rest of her body was sore from all of her lovemaking with the irrepressible Kaine too tender to wear a bra and panties. Entering the next boutique, the sales clerk recognized her and Holly instantly swore her to secrecy with money. A trick she learned from Luka.

The cool breeze welcomed her strolling along for blocks, up and down the cozy, quaint street, clearing her mind. She stopped at another boutique to have makeup applied as the store advertised for a generous purchase.

She wandered on, thinking she had survived the eye of the

Hurrikaine. Her new plan — to return to L.A., level with Brett and reject his proposal, take the bar exam and then with Lucy, open a law office.

However, her adventure to Chelsea hadn't been entirely Kaine free. Occasionally she would tune into a radio playing in a boutique, or from a passing car. She listened to Kaine's one of a kind velvet voice, the voice with no edges, singing, almost as if to call out to her.

Kaine followed Holly everywhere, like an invisible phantom stalking her. It was then she realized that perhaps because of who he was, and his highly visible profession, she would never be free of him. Even on the street corners, she found pictures of them kissing on the covers of newspapers.

There was no peace anywhere.

The memories flowed — and pictures flared in her mind.

Kaine.

Her thoughts spun, and that was the one thing she didn't want happening — to spiral out of control, as she had seven years ago, due to Jon's sudden death. She didn't want to go home and end up back in the clinic. And though she knew two things, she loved Kaine, but she hadn't healed enough to survive a headline romance with a rock star. She didn't have the experience, or the sophistication needed and she'd never dream she'd be thrown into the boiling media pot.

She'd dreamed of love coming quietly over time as it had with Jon. And apparently, the seven years hadn't been enough time to put that tragedy behind her. Luka had been so attractive and mesmerizing, and unexpected.

But Kaine was the real, sacred love, she'd carry with her for the rest of her life. His love had been the sweeter, the tender and magical type of love.

Why, had she surrendered to Luka?

Why had she sabotaged her forever love with Kaine?

The thoughts wouldn't stop assaulting her. Also, she was afraid if she ventured back into the eye of the *Hurrikaine*, she might not survive the next time. And at that moment, she realized that she'd grown. She hadn't sought the razor's edge and the blood in the sink. She was growing stronger each moment, and she was grateful that she wasn't suicidal.

It was late afternoon, the air fresh and crisp the breeze tamed. The sky, light gray, sprinkled with a few white marshmallow clouds. Perhaps the worst was over. She knew Luka would worry if she weren't in her suite when he called for her.

Watching out for reporters and the horrid paparazzi she cautiously approached the hotel. Once inside, she sprinted to her suite floor.

She froze.

Chapter Nineteen

HARD HABIT TO BREAK

Security wasn't stationed by the elevator door. Holly sensed something was wrong. From down the hall and around the corner, she unexpectedly heard the imposing British accent booming loudly.

"It's about bloody time! I sacked that incompetent lout for letting you slip out without him seeing you. Holly, what you did was so dangerous. The press. Kaine. Anything could have happened." Luka rebuked her sternly as he relieved her of a few packages.

"But it didn't." She insisted in an apologetic tone.

"Please, stop worrying. Don't be cross with me, come inside, and relax."

She placed her hand on his smooth cheek, pulled a long lock of his golden hair, and placed it lovingly behind his tiny ear.

Luka growled with discontent under his breath, but she could tell he was softening, and taking her hand from the side of his face, he kissed the palm.

"You take too many unnecessary chances."

Their eyes locked onto each other for a moment.

He was too fucking beautiful, her angel Luka.

He broke their moment, took her card key, slipped it into the slot and before he opened the door, she acknowledged his thoughtfulness.

"Thanks for the lift you left."

"I thought you might change your mind. It can be medicinal."

"It was."

"Have you ate?"

"No. I keep forgetting."

"That's it. Let's go," he ordered.

He'd changed into a dark, blue-banded-collar, cotton shirt to accent his gorgeous blue eyes, black silk vest, dark blue 501 Levi's, and brown-brushed, rough-out boots. His very long, blond hair, looked striking lying against his beautiful black leather, tailored jacket, the scent so rich that the suite reeked of leather. On his head sat a plain, black baseball cap that made him look perfectly darling. Luka never ceased to amaze her with his unbelievably fresh, good looks. The denim made him appear rough and the leather soft. How could she not wonder if his lovemaking would be a blending of contradictions — soft, yet rough?

Holly dismissed the thoughts. She didn't want to imagine how her life was going to change without Luka, and his sparkling eyes and his soft touch. It would make leaving him difficult if not impossible.

"Let's go," she agreed cheerfully.

He stepped closer.

"Thank you, Luka, for everything." She expressed as she shook her long curly mane.

"You smell lovely. Miss Holly Hill. You're the most beautiful woman in London," he said, his eyes twinkling.

His deep blue pools of gentleness almost made her blush. She held herself steady.

They dropped off the packages and then he took her hand and led her out of the suite. At the tiny sidewalk restaurant in Soho's West End, Luka insisted on sitting outside at a bistro table set. Holly didn't care where they sat, but it was clear Luka did.

It was late afternoon and a brisk and determined wind kicked up, bringing darker clouds. Struggling to forget Friar Manor, she sat sporadically entertained, watching the colorful parade of Londoners pass-by.

A mammoth, dark-gray cloud crept in to blanket the sky, slipping a veil over the lazy melon sun that peeked out, one more time before giving in to the evening's twilight.

Kaine. He popped into her mind, to remind her how he'd magically stopped the sun — but not Luka.

Holly stared at Luka. A few more hours and she would board an airliner and never look back. The reason? The dulled pain in her heart that rendered her numb, protecting her from the full measure of blame or the realization that she was traumatized from losing Kaine. It was impossible to accept that she'd poisoned their forever love.

She sighed and then slid her hand over Luka's.

"Let's go for a walk after dinner. It's much too beautiful to go back to my hotel."

"First things first, we're here to eat." Luka reminded.

"I'm not hungry." She hadn't told him she'd snuck another hit of cocaine.

"It's Chinese, everyone likes something. Order."

"Yes, sir."

The sake and orange chicken tasted great and for the first time since the dungeon with Kaine, she felt good, the hard edges melting away by the wine.

Luka asked, "You seem to be doing better."

"Thanks to you. I think the worst of the shock has faded. It will be a long time before I can reconcile what happened last night, but I'm ready to go home."

His calm blue eyes agreed, but said it was time to talk.

"I saw him today...."

"I went shopping on King's Road this afternoon. It was so nice to be out."

"He wants to apologize face-to-face."

"The salesgirls were terrific. There were times I wished I'd never have to leave Chelsea."

"He's sorry, Babe. Says he loves you. That he would never physically hurt you. He wants your forgiveness for losing his temper."

"Why are you doing this?" She demanded to know her anger growing like quicksilver then stood ready to leave.

Luka took a firm hold of her wrist and gently tugged at her, encouraging her to sit on his lap.

She did and looked at his lips, she was so close, and she could smell the orange scent on his breath.

"I agree. I don't want you near the bastard either. Remember, I'm on your side. Personally, I wanted to shove my fist down his bloody throat. But the last thing he remembers was you and me kissing in the shadows. After that, he claims he doesn't know what happened either until he woke up this morning without you."

"So ... he is at the same disadvantage I was. But he will remember and then what?"

"Not necessarily. Blackouts are common for Kaine. His are not like yours are after a long night of partying. His are different, and he's had them as long as I've known him. But since we are back on the subject of blackouts, what do you actually remember?"

"Don't you understand? I don't want to remember!" She stated emphatically and turned her head away. Because if she did remember, she would see what Kaine had — his woman, with no principle's or integrity, selfishly hiding in the shadows with Luka.

Her chin dropped.

She leaned into him. "Luka, please," she whispered.

"Can you remember? Was it Kaine, or Sarah that hurt you?"

"What's the difference? He didn't stop her."

"Maybe, he didn't know."

Luka's words stopped her cold. She relaxed in his lap. That thought was worse. Kaine didn't know? He didn't know he'd left her to crawl out of that dark Hell? Was it possible?

"Are you sure he didn't know?"

"I've known Kaine a long time, and I am hesitant, but I believe him. I can't find Sarah, she's vanished. That tells me something is off with her."

She didn't know what to think. Kaine remembered her betrayal with Luka and he still loved her. He hadn't hurt Luka. Maybe, it was about Sarah. She'd hated her on sight. But she couldn't remember. Maybe, there was hope if she could get over her feelings of shame and humiliation.

Then there was the biting fear that if their relationship ended again, it would put her back in the hospital. And where was she going to find the courage to face Kaine again? Judging from the twisting pain, she was experiencing in her chest, the panic at the thought of coming face-to-face with Kaine meant it wasn't going to be anytime soon.

Luka slipped his arms around her waist, he looked into her eyes, and she could see he was trying to find the right words.

"What is it, Luka? You're scaring me."

He kissed her lips quickly, then dropped his chin a moment as if he was struggling to find the right words. He looked up at her.

"I'm so sorry to be a messenger in this. I could only get CMT to let you pull out of your contract early, with one condition. You're big news, Babe. Your romance with Kaine is already worldwide headlines."

"What are you saying?"

"In less than an hour, you're expected to do the final interview for the CMT contest."

"I'm okay. I can do an interview." She exhaled a giant breath of relief.

"You don't understand. CMT wants to interview you with Kaine ... alone."

The panic arrived, again, slamming into Holly's stomach and a wave of nausea washed over her, hitting hard, threatening to force the bites of dinner she'd eaten up to her throat. The humiliation, too intense, too fresh. She couldn't face Kaine knowing what she'd done. She jumped up from Luka's lap to run, but he blocked her exit with his arm, slamming her back against his chest, quickly wrapping his arms around her and held her in place.

He spoke reassuringly into her ear. "Holly, Babe, you have to see him."

Holly clung to Luka's chest. "I can't see him," she protested laced with embarrassment.

Nausea struck resulting in a profound and unadulterated feeling of shame. She pleaded with her eyes to Luka, not to make her do it. Hot tears welled in her eyes, threatening to spill.

His thumb moved quickly to rescue each falling tear.

"Don't Babe, I can't take it when you look at me this way."

Holly pulled Luka closer, and she draped her hand over his shoulder. She drank in the comfort Luka openly offered to her. When she relaxed, she glanced to the side and then across the street.

Her eyes locked on to the sad, rejected blue eyes of — Kaine — his pale face, haggard, his eyes full of fear and loneliness, but mostly disbelief. He spun on his heels and entered the building.

Kaine, dressed as the perfect black knight, wearing a long, black, velvet coat and black trousers. His brown hair flowed around his shoulders. She heard the cracking of her heart again. He'd caught her in Luka's arms, again — fuck!

Holly shook her head in distress, then defiance.

"Luka, I can't. Let CMT sue me. I can't face that man ever again."

He held her lovingly, allowing her to draw from his invincible strength. He placed his cheek against her cheek to calm her and in a relaxed and even tone told her.

"I'll find a way to appease CMT."

He dropped pound notes on the table.

"Come on Babe, let's walk. You have to get him out of your system and then get the hell out of London. We have a date to watch the sunset in California. We have a future," he promised to encourage her.

"Luka, I have knots in my stomach the size of beach balls," she complained as her anxiety climbed to stratospheric heights. She reached out and gripped his hand lost in a state of panic.

"I understand but remember last night, you only showed me your true feelings. That's what's eating at Kaine."

Luka's eyes flashed with concern and then he pulled her to him and held her close. His body trembled when he pressed her to fill the curves of his body with hers.

Luka hugged her. He kissed her lips easily and then dropped his arm around her waist.

"Let's take that walk?"

His last memory was of you and me kissing.

Why on Earth, would Kaine want her back?

Chapter Twenty

A WOMAN IN LOVE
(IT'S NOT ME)

Hopeless. That was the sinking feeling. This had to be what outlaws experienced when drug out to be hanged, the only suitable ending for a convicted criminal. She knew her crimes against Kaine and the shame burned, rushing in her veins, faster than the incredible cocaine she'd done from Luka's private stash. How could she even think about Kaine?

She looked at Luka. And she didn't see him with her usual, consuming lust and desire. She saw him with her heart, her soul. She did love Luka so, but not like Kaine.

We have a date to watch the sunset in California.

We have a future.

Resigned to stop obsessing about Kaine she believed Luka to be right. He was her future because he was her partner in the crime. She locked her arms around Luka's waist, holding on for dear life.

"Why do you put up with me Luka? I can only bring you misery."

"You let me be the judge."

"You deserve better than I can give you," she challenged remembering Kaine's accusatory words.

Even he doesn't deserve you.

Luka stopped, pulled her into his chest, hugged her lovingly, and whispered into her hair. "I understand how hard it is for you to give now. You need time to pull out of this emotional nosedive. Time will help and thousands of miles away from him will help even more. And sorry to contradict you, but it's I that doesn't deserve you." Then he pressed her head against his chest.

"I hope you're right about the time," she countered.

"When haven't I been?"

She felt him smile.

Outside her suite's door, Luka gave the security man a break. He took a step closer to her, letting his body push against her. The cocaine she'd snorted in the elevator was starting to energize her, propelling her to touch Luka and she knew what that meant. And so did Luka. She needed to leave London having experienced Luka's touch, love, his memory — not Kaine.

Holly went up on her toes and slid her hands up the outside of his jacket. To her surprise, Luka's soft, scented lips, kissed her back lightly, then harder, as if it would be a long time before they kissed again. She'd met no resistance as she searched his mouth, their tongues dancing in a perfect rhythm only they knew. Luka kissed her a sweet kiss and then evolved into a fierce kiss as if lost in time and he was bringing her with him. Luka leaned her up against the wall pushing his hips into her.

She'd given up thoughts of making love to him. Luka

Hunter had been so maddening, too many times. And the loneliness covered her like the London fog, thick and clinging as Luka pulled away.

"Let's go inside, Babe," he coaxed quietly.

If this had been Kaine, she'd be filled with joy and anticipation, knowing they would soon make amazing love.

However, this was Luka — it could never be.

He smiled and winked at her.

Encouraged, Holly turned and opened the door. Before she entered the room, she knew. Before she turned on the lights, she knew. The air was thick, pungent with the familiar scent.

Luka confirmed her suspicions when he flipped on the light to expose her suite covered in roses. Everywhere. Every space covered with beautiful vases filled with red roses, dozens, and dozens.

Landfall — Kaine struck again.

"No, no, no...." she muttered.

Luka stretched his arms around her waist to embrace her.

"Luka, how can he? He knows what I've done. Why won't he go away? Why me?"

"Because he's Kaine. He's spoiled. He's used to getting his way and what he wants. He wants you. For the first time in his life, he saw a real future with a woman, you, Babe." He stated matter-of-factly.

She sensed he was not smiling. Bittersweet tears ran down her cheeks as she turned to look up into Luka's sad eyes, eyes that wore the white flag of defeat.

"Come here." Luka encouraged as he sat on the end of the bed and patted the mattress beside him for her to sit.

"You ask me why you. I can try to explain what is

happening here." But first, he wiped away a tear falling from her cheek and then took her hand in his.

"Remember earlier when you told me about Brett?"

"Brett, what does he have to do with any of this?"

"He doesn't directly. Listen, Babe, you already have a working understanding of what Brett needs if he decides to seek public office and how to do that. He needs to have a particular type of woman or wife. He has charm, money, a strong reputation, and his love of work, which are essential ingredients for his success. What he sees in you is your loyalty and dedication to the job — and that's him. He may be a lawyer with an appetite for becoming a politician, but he is a salesman. His product is selling ideas of justice and fairness and that makes him a businessman first.

"Kaine and I are not any different. We are both businessmen first. Our product is selling a dream, an image — we sell love. We sell love with songs on records. We use performance, live concerts, videos, and lastly publicity. As younger men, we got caught up in the act of the music scene. Now, we create the act. Now, the focus is selling clean, family friendly, love songs.

"Usually, the types of women we come into contact with are either what you saw backstage that are too young or is self-centered like Claudine. We seldom are exposed to the women in-between them. This is also a time in our lives where we are doing well financially, having homes, material comforts. We are looking to spend more time with a particular woman. We are looking for a reliable woman, not a girl. A woman that is intelligent, able to challenge and comfort us. We want to be able to respect her, love her and she has to be down-to-earth and nurturing to be the mother of our children.

"For men like Kaine and I, we also have to factor in that family means there will be heirs to vast fortunes and as you well know, that means solicitors. This woman, to become a wife, will need to not only be able to manage the household and upbringing of the children but understand that we are businessmen first. We can't be as hands-on as we'd both prefer. Perhaps later, but not now.

"Kaine is a smart and astute businessman. We both have joint and separate business ventures — we run empires. We need a formally educated, professional woman that has a working knowledge of the types of demands on our time and to understand the commitments that come with running these empires. That special woman needs to be independent and lastly, she has to be able to love us, accept the lifestyle, and understand its harsh demands.

"Many times, we've talked at length about this subject. Kaine never accepted this bloody amazing woman existed. That was why I told you that Kaine would never marry. Then one day, a woman showed up wearing a business suit to a *Hurrikaine* concert. He saw you backstage and that told both Kaine and I a number of things. You were not like any others. You were a bit older, had to be both educated and a professional. The fact that you're beautiful was icing. Your past, well, let's say the celibacy wasn't required, but because of your tragedy, what it brought to us, was your inspiration for a fresh start. You, Babe, were a woman we could see ourselves married to for the rest of our lives.

"What made you special to me was you'd also met me outside of my world and looked at me with those adoring eyes that wanted me without all my hundreds of strings. I know

Kaine found the same eyes. I captured them on film. You weren't as impressed with what he was — a rock star — more with who he was. It may seem to you that everything moved too fast, but you see now, we both knew exactly what we were looking for in a woman. That's why once we each realized — separately — that 'it' was you — our relationships became instantly complicated and evolved into a rivalry. Neither of us ever discussed that a special woman would become the one we both would want."

Kaine had told her the same thing. That the romance wasn't moving fast. He'd known what he was looking for, he'd been waiting for her.

But Luka was still talking.

"You Babe … you're the special woman. You have shown that you respect yourself more than the idea of being a girlfriend of a wealthy, famous, rock star. You did that today when you walked away from him last night. You're riddled with guilt, and it's not because you think you'd lost him, but because you believed you're no good for him. How do you think that makes him feel? How I feel? You put his feelings before yours. What that means to me … and I bloody hate saying these words, I was wrong, Babe. You're in love with him. The kind of love I want from you.

"I know because of his rough treatment of you if it even happened. Harsh treatment never stopped any women before you. Women took anything he had to give, pain or pleasure. That's why he's been holed up in the castle for so long. He's like me, gave up on any ideas of real love and family. All of these reasons I've explained are why he will come for you. He knows his chances of finding another you, to love and love him, are next to bloody impossible. And that's also, why I want to spend a thousand sunsets with you. I know if it happens, it will be me you want, not my money, my status, or me as a trophy. Though, you seemed to want me. And that is the biggest turn-on for men like Kaine and me.

"As far as Kaine goes, he knows what it's like to love you and have that genuine love returned. He will regret whatever happened between the two of you last night, most, if not all of his life. And he doesn't even remember it. He knows he lost you. How does the pathetic bastard live with that?"

She was glad she was sitting. She would never have thought her selfish and insensitive actions could be interpreted in such a gracious manner. And for Luka to confess he'd thought she'd proved that she was in love with Kaine. Those were unbelievable words she'd never expected to hear from him.

"I know you think you're speaking a sort of truth," she argued. "But Luka, I still don't understand why any of this has happened. I'm not special. I not only broke Kaine's trust and respect with my behavior with you but yours by running off and staying with Kaine. Why at this point either of you would want anything to do with me or be able to trust me again, I find the thought to be preposterous. I don't believe I deserve either of you," she heartily insisted. Tears dripped from her eyes and she heard Kaine's horrible words in the corridor.

Now I can never trust you.

Her heart ached from the stabbing pain of his indictment against her. And then she realized that he didn't remember saying those words to her. He'd trusted her, to come back to him.

"Babe, trust is built. Sometimes one step forward and two

steps back. And by your own words that you don't deserve us, tells men like us, it's our well-being you're looking out for, not yours. Again, realize all the money and prestige that is involved with men like us. You saw the headlines. We usually never know why women are with us. In the past, we used to hope it was for us, but hope had been destroyed a long time ago. I believe both Kaine and I had decided to live out the rest of our lives with meaningless relationships to fill the time and our needs. I more than him. He locked himself up in the castle. But open our hearts. Not so bloody much."

She noticed that was the first time that Luka had mentioned that the castle belonged to Kaine. She assumed though he'd think Emily brought her up to speed — and she had.

"You see, I do understand Kaine. Why he is so fucked up right now, filled with guilt and regret about something he can't even remember. To have offered marriage to you, for Kaine, well that is one for the books. I never believed he would ever go that far. But he did with you. That is why you *were* the Heart of the *Hurrikaine*."

He had to stop talking. She couldn't take much more. Holly couldn't stop the tears. It was much worse than she realized, especially when he'd said *were.*

"Men like us look at the bigger picture. We run a business, wife, and then children. They are a delicate balance. Something I don't believe either of us thought we would ever be concerned about putting into place. Trust, well, it would seem he wants to rebuild it with you. That's why he wanted to see you face-to-face. You and I, we have the gift of time Kaine didn't have. I've been telling you all along I understood your predicament. I knew I could wait. Kaine and I have shared women in the past, so your affair with him, I could handle it. I'm not jealous of Kaine, like that. He has his demons, and I have mine. Sometimes, I'm sorry you met either of us. I knew what you were getting into, you didn't. What I truly admired about you — how you followed your heart."

Holly couldn't wrap her thoughts around all of his words. But she understood that both men had always been so far ahead of her. They'd planned her life with them and she couldn't see past the moment. She finally understood how much Kaine overcame to love her. All of them had to overcome so many challenges of their past to love each other.

She heard Luka sigh as he bent in close and lightly brushed her lips with his. She knew it was time.

He squeezed her hand and apologized. "I shouldn't leave you alone like this. Especially now, but I'm...." Luka didn't finish his sentence.

Holly understood he'd opened up to explain because even Luka seemed stunned by Kaine's overwhelming demonstration of love, but nothing else changed.

"You're needed." She reminded without resentment, understanding that his dedication was part of what attracted her to him.

"I need time to think. And I'm not alone Luka. I have all these beautiful roses to keep me company."

Holly heard Luka muttering as he surveyed the roses covering the suite, shaking his head.

"I'll be damned. Kaine's bloody deep in love ... poor fucker."

He spoke up louder. "I'll ring you in the morning to take you to the airport."

He wasn't staying.

Luka turned, flicked back a long lock of his hair over his shoulder and leaned in and gave her another quick peck on her lips while pressing a new vial into her hand.

Luka Hunter got up from the bed, turned, straightened his shoulders, and walked out the door, leaving her with her roses and memories of better times and never looked back.

Holly meandered around the room tending to her magnificent rose garden, welcoming every flower. Each soft, velvet petal, expressed Kaine's forever love for her.

Thirsty, she popped open a beer and added a slice of lime. She looked at the stack of phone messages. There was an impressive stack from Brett. He was furious, and she wasn't surprised. She'd forgotten him. He'd understand when she filled him in on what had happened. There were, at least, ten messages from newspapers and rag magazines, eight from Kaine, six from Solange, six from Emily, one from Ian, and one from John? John Roberts?

She wasn't sure what her next step was. Her plan was hazy at best. But for the first time, in a long time, she had a glimmer of how it all happened. Why Luka took to her so quickly and why Kaine had done the same. It was what Brett saw in her so long ago. The steady, loyal woman and it seemed they all wanted that from her, though, stable, was not a term she would use to describe her recent behavior. She'd been erratic, confused and inconsistent, and, in the end, disloyal, a betrayer, and a cheat.

She recalled all the times she'd caught Kaine watching her. He saw his future with her, planned their life. He'd truly wanted the children. He'd seen enough women in his lifetime to know what he wanted when he'd found her. He'd wanted her from the first moment he'd discovered her backstage rejected by Luka.

She couldn't keep up this line of thought because she would surely find a way to Paris with Kaine, instead of L.A. with Luka.

And what of Luka? There on the streets of Chelsea, he'd seen a glimpse of having a woman attracted to him, his beauty and then later his gentleness, and thoughtfulness. How patient he had been with her. To know all along that any happiness he would have with her would be at Kaine's expense. It had to affect the always strong Luka Hunter.

She started to pack her few belongings in the bag Luka brought. Then on the way to the airport, she planned to pick up more luggage.

After enjoying a thin line of cocaine, she headed for the closet. There she discovered her long, leather coat in a garment bag along with her suit that apparently started it all, the white mini skirt and tailored jacket she'd worn to the concert. There were slacks, blouses, the trendy, black, lace dress Kaine bought for her at the Asset boutique and then practically ripped from her during the passionate ride home from Wembley. And the LV satchel, and an extra piece — a Louis Vuitton Keepall, and a black hard-shelled guitar case.

She pulled them both out and placed them on the bed.

Inside the Keepall by her sexy lingerie neatly folded, her toiletries, and the letterman *Hurrikaine* band jacket he had given her. She found the unused lollipops with a scribbled note.

No need for these without you.

There was a large manila envelope stuffed with newspaper clippings highlighting their brief, headline-stopping affair. His portable CD player was tucked inside with the Roberts CD's and another note.

Play this and remember the best of me.

It became more and more difficult to see through her welling tears. She turned to the black hard-shelled guitar case, opened it and there laid, Slick. Beside him, a piece of hotel embossed notepaper filled with Kaine's precious lyrics — the song he'd written for her "My Lady" with the last note.

Holly, My Dearest Lady Love.
I don't understand why you have to leave me.
Know I'll always love you, My Lady.
Wherever, in the world, I go and sing this song.
I will remember you.
Take care of Slick. He's the best of me.
And I want you to have that.
Love always, your forever man.

Her hand crawled up to the back of her neck and she massaged the knotted muscles. She burst into a sob when her heart shattered apart. It was finally finished. Kaine had been humble and gracious and sent her his beautiful goodbye. She slumped to the floor beside the bed crying from an unbearable searing chest pain.

She read the lyrics again, hearing his sweet, breathy voice singing to her, remembering how she'd laid wrapped in his arms backstage at Friar Manor. She crawled over to the CD player and turned on the Roberts CD. He started to sing of their forever love. She chugged more beer, one after the other, hoping to dull the burning pain. She cried until her shattered heart was empty and could cry no more.

She had no interest in what time it was.

Holly picked up Kaine's band jacket, thick with the scent of his cologne, slipped beneath the covers, and pulled the jacket to cuddled up inside it. Soon she would be home, alone in the canyon and he would be alone in Europe.

The only difference, she understood why he'd loved her so deeply, so fast.

Chapter Twenty-One

LOVE SONG

What a mess everything was. She clamped her eyelids shut, trying to force herself to drift off to sleep. But merciful sleep would not come. Paris, France, thousands of miles apart, the torture, started again, dreaming of Paris.

"Babe…"

"Luka?" she asked, answering the private cellular phone.

"I wish you were here."

"I came back and I'm next door in the pub. I shouldn't have left you."

Yes!

She wouldn't be alone with nothing but tormenting memories and crushing disappointment.

She spoke softly, not sure, of the right thing to say.

"I think after your explanation, we need each other tonight, more than ever. But since I understand Luka, I can't promise anything."

"Neither can I Babe, neither can I," he replied with a tone of no hope or promise.

Holly hung up bewildered, hoping this wasn't another colossal mistake. Luka's enlightening talk, Kaine's gifts, along with his poetic goodbye, upset her to her core.

Luka appeared, leaning in the doorway.

Holly lunged at him, causing her to fall straight into his welcoming arms. She marveled at the formidable power she drew from him.

Holly spoke with tears streaming. "What are we doing to each other Luka?"

"All we can Babe." And he hugged her as if she would evaporate at any moment.

She eyed his sweet, comforting lips, wanting to taste them.

Luka did not disappoint her. He picked her up so gently, kicking the door shut with his foot. He walked swiftly to the bed and then laid her down like a prized doll.

Warm, sensuous lips closed over hers with such gentle expertise that her body trembled with anticipation. Luka was rekindling the desires that had grown calm from her demoralizing encounter with Kaine.

This was Luka.

They kissed with a frantic need, knowing the other was there to satisfy until the immediate urgency passed.

Holly broke the kiss first to look at him. He had to see it in her eyes that this was wrong. That this was goodbye to him too. That everything that had started in London had to end in London.

Luka kissed her quickly, his eyes welling with redness. His traitorous thoughts made him glance away from her for a moment but maintained in a whisper.

"Not tonight, Babe. Tonight of all nights, we need to

comfort each other. It's like we're waiting for the shadow of death, to cross over our doorway."

Holly forced a weak smile, a bit dramatic, even from Luka, but it summed up the situation.

Buzzed from her last blast of cocaine, she leaned over him to swallow half a muscle relaxer with a gulp of mineral water.

He spoke with caution, "Please don't send me away, instead, why don't you soak? I have a few people I need to contact."

She nodded weakly. The sadness was massive. The ghost of Kaine hung thick, like an impenetrable veil between them.

"All right, but try to hurry," she encouraged her tone flat.

She looked over her shoulder to see him pulling out his phone.

The cool water lapped about her body as she stood. The hour passed fast. She stepped out and wrapped herself in a towel. Her body still ached as if she'd barely survived boot camp, instead of the landfall of the *Hurrikaine*. She brushed her teeth, groomed her long hair, tossing it up into a ponytail.

She entered the suite.

Darkness.

She heard the deep breathing of an exhausted, wonderful man, who didn't deserve her reeling off an impetuous five-day love affair.

Luka had devoted himself to her since their first meeting, but then when life ever the way she'd was planned it?

Holly walked over to the window, pulled back the curtain, and discovered the sky lit by the moon that looked like a giant light bulb hanging high.

She turned and pulled Slick from his case, sat on the settee and played her song, "Cold Without You" her every thought mourning the loss of Kaine. After a while, the silence became deafening, and her thoughts turned to Luka.

Holly ambled over to him, her heart pounding in her chest. She wasn't sure she could sleep beside him because any second, she would melt like the wax of a candle to fit his flawless body and want him badly. Shards of pale moonlight highlighted his gorgeous face that slept like poetry. His long, golden hair fanned about the pillows, his perfectly arched eyebrows, the crescent shape of his tawny eyelashes, took her breath away, leaving a special brand on her heart.

This was fucking impossible! How could she sleep with him? She glanced at his shirt, vest, and Levi's in a pile, his socks and then randomly tossed boots. His jacket and baseball cap were thrown on the floor. She deserved this cruel and unusual punishment, wondering what kind of love he would be for the rest of her life.

She moved closer to him.

Mmmm.

He laid naked under the white sheet that barely covered his waist. Her eyes followed the sharp line of his rugged chest, so muscular, but no buff. She admired his golden mat of hair, sparkling against his tanned chest from the moonlight. Her eyes followed the slight, thin trail of hair down his abdomen, to the edge of the sheet and inches below to the large swelling. She momentarily entertained the luscious thoughts of him full-sized, setting fires that burned on top of each other until her every nerve ending sizzled. She shook her head wondering how exquisite Luka would feel. No man should be allowed to be this alluring and sensual, it wasn't fair. But she knew there was no love for them tonight.

Nothing was fair.

Holly dropped the towel, slipped beneath the sheet. She pressed her body into the folds of his feverish, hot body. She fought her fingertips from caressing him, rolling them into small balls and leaned into him.

He quietly responded, with a long breath steeped in his alluring scent. His top arm naturally coiled around her, his other hand inserted itself under her and then moved down stopping on her derrière. Luka pulled her hips to him with ease, placing his top thigh between hers. His semi-erect arousal planted next to her belly made her conjure up deliciously wicked thoughts.

In a sleepy, husky voice, Luka whispered.

"Come closer to me, Babe. You're safe. I can control myself."

Holly smiled a bittersweet smile, exhaled a long ragged gasp as Luka's warm breath feathered her cheek. She was helplessly drawn to this sleeping beauty. She briefly pressed her lips to Luka's parted, succulent lips that always begged her to kiss them again, and again, so sorry she would leave him too.

He didn't respond.

"Sweet Luka," she whispered.

Was that a smile she saw curling at the corners of his lips?

Chapter Twenty-Two

YOU GOT LUCKY

Day 7

Where was she?

Holly awoke, disoriented and confused.

The pain arrived quickly.

Alone— no Kaine. The ugly truth rushed in like an avalanche smothering her in her evil and unforgivable betrayal. The tears dropped with no control to stop them. She snuggled into Luka's embrace.

The longing for Kaine, his arms, his scent, his love grew unbearable and needed quenching. Instead, here lay Luka. But her body yearned for Kaine and burned her alive, and so she cried, lost without Kaine.

Holly watched Luka sleeping, knowing there wasn't a way to make love with him, even if his potent elixir would stop the aching pain of wanting Kaine. Here she was her last morning in London and the burning ache for Kaine would not fade. No such luck, she was condemned, and the fire grew more intense and the tight grasp of betrayal followed on its heels threatened to force her to the cold bathroom floor.

No, she wouldn't do that.

Not again.

Not this time.

Holly had taken for granted she would awaken with Kaine and have her every fantasy quenched by his insatiable desire for her.

She should be thrilled.

She'd be traveling to Paris, about to be married within hours. Why was it when she was near the commitment stage of marriage, disaster struck? She hid her face recalling Jon and the plane, Brett and setting the wedding date that ended due to this disastrous trip to London, but with Kaine — it was Luka.

How like a *Hurrikaine*, her life had become, the directions quickly changing. She wasn't with Kaine joyously packing to leave for Paris. Instead, here was Luka, his beautiful golden hair spread about her pillows like a shimmering waterfall. She twisted a long lock of his golden hair about her fingers. She lay listening to him breathe long and deep. There was the easiness an unexplained comfort zone with Luka. She pressed her fingertips to his chest. She thought she might count the beat of his heart. A heart that said he loved her too. How many times had he proved that to her?

She continued to cry. She reminisced back to a time long ago in the hospital and how many months it had taken her to stop the crying.

How long would it take now?

Luka stirred.

His hot body coiled his arms around her tighter, pulling the length of her into alignment with his. His hands slowly wandered all over her trembling body. He was doing it again, creating a burning caress, tempting her to plead for his mercy. Her breath quickened inhaling the morning scent of him.

Luka opened his eyes a crack and his sexy baby blues sparkled.

"You look more exquisite by the morning light, lying naked in my arms than I ever imagined," he whispered with a sleepy, husky tone.

Holly nestled into him while he pulled her down into a swift current of desire.

"You've pictured me naked in the morning?" she teased.

"Since I first laid eyes on you."

"I pictured you too." She shyly revealed.

"I hope I haven't disappointed you?"

"Why would you say that?" she asked exhaling a ragged breath.

"You haven't ravaged my body. I must be losing my charm."

He pulled her closer.

"What's this about, Babe?" He raised his hand to wipe away her tears.

"I can't... Not yet, not..." Holly moved in closer, pushing her thigh firmly against his and turned her chin up waiting to taste his lips.

"I am not going to abandon you. I am not suddenly going to leave you as Jon did — as Kaine has. I promise I won't do that to you."

And in seconds, Luka took her hard and fast.

Luka — rested.

Holly surrendered to the turbulent sensations that assaulted her, and she smiled with anticipation, as his hands roamed her gently, easily, drawing her bruised body even closer to his.

Only her moans of pleasure broke the electrified silence. How well he touched her body.

How perfectly his hand slid between her legs to dip into the satiny wet heat of her body. Her breath quickly changed to a steady pant.

Between volleys of unrestrained kisses, Luka whispered.

"I want to wake up with you, every morning for the rest of my life."

Luka's lips consumed her, becoming incredibly noisy, moving in the same maddening rhythm as his fingers. Slow and deliberate, in and out, he plunged over and over again.

Her hands roamed his body with an adventurous new freedom because he'd never allowed her this close to him.

He'd never been naked.

Quickly her hand traveled downward. With a new excitement as if pulled into a whirlpool of swirling lust.

Luka gave her permission to go ahead. He would let her love him. To her delight, she discovered more of him that she'd remembered and wrapped her hand around his growing hard desire. This panther-like man consumed her with indescribable sensations as if swept along a dark swirling abyss.

Luka released her mouth, then her body and pulled his fingers from her as the heady rapture, fanned her burning desires.

She delivered a flurry of wet kisses to his neck, then chest, heading straight for him growing hard in her hand. She wanted to see him and show him her intense feelings for him — her sweet Luka.

But then — it wasn't Luka she wanted.

She glanced up at him.

His beautiful fucking blue eyes-to-die for were closed, his face a flushed color awaiting her pleasure. His arms were folded behind his head with his hands tucked beneath the pillow. His golden chest rose and fell with each labored breath. The delicious sight of Luka Hunter naked and aroused should have been more than she could take.

But the hated cellular phone rang.

"No...." she cried out.

The horrid technology squashed the sounds of their newly promised desires. If she was going to do this with Luka, it had to be these moments, before she stopped to think about what she was doing.

She needed him.

She feared he would answer.

Luka didn't move.

Neither did she.

Luka leaned over on the fourth ring and answered. It was as if he had struck her face with the back of his hand, his rejection so potent. Everyone — needed him more than her.

Holly rolled away from Luka.

She couldn't look him in the eyes and tried to block out the one-sided conversation. She drew her knees inward.

In the end, he'd agreed to something, but as possibilities of their wonderful moments passed, she understood, he had somewhere to be soon. Someone else needed him more than she did.

Disheartened, she rolled off the bed and stood while Luka listened to the caller on the other end of the line. She glanced over at him. She shook her head so filled with disappointment. Again, the betrayal seeped in inside her. She was using Luka. Leading him on knowing there was no future for them.

What the hell had happened to her?

Holly was disgusted with herself.

Luka sat naked to his waist, looking more beautiful than any Greek god possibly could. The sheet half covered his enlarged awakening, the golden curls peeked out over the edge of the sheet, his long, lean legs were uncovered.

Luka finished his call and laid still. His calm blue eyes were content to watch her finish dressing.

Holly didn't miss his strength growing strong beneath the sheet. The simplest of routines were the ultimate in sensually.

It was time to dress, and she zipped up her new pair of chocolate-colored slacks and pulled on a new black *Hurrikaine* sweatshirt Luka brought in the bag. All she wanted to do was strip and make love, but not here, not now, and not with him.

Her mind betrayed her with sporadic, sizzling memories of making love with Kaine. The flashing thoughts of when she and Kaine had been rising comets that made the world stand up and take notice of their flagrant love affair. Together, their love set the world on fire, yet they'd burned out as quickly.

"I've got to shower, Babe."

"That sounds wonderful," she said as she sat down to take off her pants.

"I mean a cold shower — and, alone," he explained in his tone of don't argue with me.

"I want to do this right Babe. Fate has kept us apart again

and I don't want us to become like the others in my life."

He was right.

Holly had almost given in and ruined her plans. She'd spoken out of turn about the shower. She needed to go home and put London behind her.

And, unfortunately, Luka misunderstood because he struggled to explain.

"I do want you. I do not deny that I want to fu... make love to you more than any woman I've ever known. You're different Holly … you're a sweet poison in my blood, I can't find an antidote for — and, I don't want anymore. Can't you see in my eyes how I feel? If anything Babe, I want you too much." He confessed, straightening his back as he sat up, his voice thick and husky, the sheet inching lower.

"But I also want you to look at me the way you did our first day together in Chelsea, before the bloody video shoot at the Hard Rock. What I don't want is any lingering ghost between us. I don't want you to prove anything to yourself. I want your memories of me in London to be honorable, and happy. Not clouded and tainted by Kaine's rejection.

"I can see you're devastated and lost by Kaine suddenly abandoning you. It's a reminder of Jon and how quickly he left you. And that reminds you that things can change within minutes. I know that pain, and I want you to believe that I will never abandon you. When Kaine is out of your system, I promise, you will find out all about me.

"Remember, we're lucky, Babe. We have the gift of time. We will have thousands of sunsets to get to know each other. Be patient my love."

Holly didn't miss it. His words are powerful — *my love*.

Luka slipped from beneath the sheet as she closed her eyes. She opened them quick enough to catch the backside of him vanish into the bathroom. How perfect his body, the smooth line of his shoulder blades, his waist narrowing to the bright suntan line on his slim hips. The pale color of his rounded cheeks, the muscles flexing beneath his tight skin made her drop her chin to her chest, shaking her head, closing her eyes.

What was she going to do about Luka?

While Luka showered, her torment continued. She fought the pictures of the water dripping down his hard shaft. She bit her lips daydreaming how a man with his powerful size would fit inside her. However, Luka was spot on with his evaluation. No use trying to ignore Kaine, he stood in the suite, standing tall and handsome between her and Luka.

Luka was right. He'd known the ghost of Kaine was here.

Driven to wrap the red roses separately in newspapers that tracked her incredible love affair, she squeezed all that she could into her new suitcase.

When Holly was ready to leave for the airport, she sat waiting and pulled out the vial. She sipped a cup of English Breakfast Tea and waited for Luka with her memories.

Luka came out dressed only in his Levi's, the top two buttons yet to be fastened. He was drying his hair with a towel. The flush of his love drained with the cold water. He dropped the towel and combed his hair back with his fingers. His face more handsome than she'd ever seen him, a full day's growth of beard grew in a few shades darker. He walked over close to her. His scent arrived first from the lavender body wash and shampoo and then he bent down to kiss her, bringing a waft of his breath, minty fresh and inviting, as it blew across her face.

"Don't be angry with me." He pleaded.

She moved to kiss him, then thought no, and instead allowed her hand to take a quick trip across his damp bare chest.

"Please, Babe, you're doing it again. Wait for L.A."

No, she wasn't going to wait for L.A., the new plan had not changed. She would never see Luka again. Her spirit flattened, her fairy tale world had ended. This dream would finish with Luka.

Holly had a plane to catch.

She got up and darted into the bathroom to brush her teeth and hair.

"Babe?" Luka appealed to her, wiping away the cheerful smile on his face when she reentered the room.

"I hope you can forgive me, but you're going to have to go to the airport alone. I have to locate some expensive video equipment and make sure it finds its way to the airport."

She stood in the bathroom doorframe. It would make it easier to say goodbye. But Luka was leaving, and it wasn't the way she'd planned to end with him. The thought that this was the final goodbye pushed the tears to cascade down her cheeks.

"Babe?"

"I'm not strong Luka, and things have been an awful mess for too long now."

"You'll be fine. You're stronger than you think, Babe."

Maybe he was right, she would find out soon.

He stopped and pointed with his head to the new piece of luggage.

"Where did that come from, Babe?" He slipped on the denim shirt, leaving the front opened looking as if he was half-undressed and getting ready to make love, instead of half-dressed getting ready to leave her.

"Kaine sent over my belongings from the penthouse." She clarified, eyeing his chest that usually invited her touch.

There was a time when she would have welcomed the suggestion to finish unbuttoning his pants. But her heart was not in it. She *was* the Heart of the *Hurrikaine,* but she was going home.

"He sent you Slick?" His voice rose, surprised as he surveyed the guitar case. His eyebrows clashed in the middle of his forehead.

"Kaine seems to think Slick is better off with me."

"He never gives away guitars. He loves them almost as much as he loves himself."

Holly ignored the dripping sarcasm. She didn't respond.

"Don't think about the past, Babe. Try to focus on warm beaches and sprawling sunsets. Our bright future and our life together will be so different once we're out of the fucking eye of the *Hurrikaine*. I can make you happy. I promise...."

She didn't want to hear about promises. Promises could be broken. She would say what was needed for him to let her go today. And that would be it. When he returned to L.A., she would not be available.

She sauntered over to Luka.

"You have already made me happy." She surrendered herself to him, as more tears spilled out and down her cheeks as she clung to him, letting her hands slip under his shirt to roam his flesh. He'd been her only friend during this ordeal.

"How did I get so lucky?" He wondered half-aloud, kissing the shell of her ear. "I'm glad I make you happy," he said.

Luka looked deep into her eyes, revealing his love, so

vibrant, and energetic. She watched the tip of his pink tongue pass quickly over his bottom lip. That meant he was going to kiss her to oblivion.

Instead, Luka released her. He buttoned his shirt, and tucked it in, and finished buttoning the top buttons of his pants.

For once, she was thankful there would be no kisses.

He slipped into the leather jacket, crushed the baseball hat on his head. He checked the suite clock and then picked up the Louis Vuitton Keepall from Kaine. She held on to Slick and her other suitcase.

They stepped out into the corridor. Luka sent the security man ahead to make sure the car was waiting for them downstairs. When the security man was out of sight, Luka immediately sat the LV Keepall down on the floor. And as if an uncontrollable urge he drew her into his arms. His mouth closed over hers before she could think to react, pressing her passionately. She dropped the things in her hands. She never heard the thud as she surrendered, reveling in Luka's exploding need for her. She wrapped her arms around his neck pushed her hips into him and wrapped her leg around his.

"Do you think it's possible that we could fall in love?" he whispered.

"There are those sunsets you speak of, Angel Eyes."

"Maybe, like you loved Kaine?"

"No. I don't love you like Kaine." And what she didn't say, *that is the forever love.*

"You can say you're *in* love with me?" His eyes read as if he doubted this miracle could happen to him.

"Yes, I do love you, Luka."

There it was again and breaking her heart because this love

for him would never grow because she *is* the Heart of the *Hurrikaine*.

"Then I will make you forget him." He hugged her tighter.

"Say those words one more time, so I'll have something to dream on until I see you in L.A."

"I do love you, Angel Eyes."

She kissed Luka hard and slid her arms up his broad shapely shoulders. Her fingers ran deep into his damp, silky hair. Then, as quickly she opened her eyes and gazed into his, she realized Luka dropped his guard. He was letting her see, his unconditional love. How well he'd restrained his feelings for her because his eyes were set ablaze with passion. Luka, her beautiful Prince Charming, hugged her as if she was his future.

But she wasn't.

This was goodbye.

Holly was about to kiss him one last time, something distracted her and caused her to glance over his shoulder to the elevator. The car doors closed, but not before she saw the long, black, velvet, coat — the long, dark hair — the sad, rejected blue eyes.

Holly snapped. She must have been seeing things. Within a blink of her eyes, the elevator doors closed. But the potent moment hung heavy in the air.

"Holly, what's wrong?"

"Nothing." She insisted. "A ghost following me."

Holly struggled to break free from Luka. Then picked up Slick, and her suitcase and headed down the corridor to the elevator. When the car arrived, Holly and Luka entered.

Instantly, she stepped into the mist, surrounded by the scent of his cologne.

She'd seen Kaine!

Why had he been there?

Why had he left?

Of course. He saw them together. Standing locked in another passionate embrace, as she confessed her love to Luka, not knowing it was her saying goodbye.

By the time Holly entered the lobby, she had noticed Luka never mentioned Kaine's cologne in the elevator.

Neither had she.

She'd regained her composure and headed toward the main desk.

"Miss Hill." The concierge called out. "A tall gentleman asked me to hand this package to you personally before you checked out."

He laid a twelve by eighteen inches, gold-foil box, tied with another three inches wide, black satin ribbon in her hands.

"Thank you. Did you get his name?"

We all know his name.

"He said you would know."

Yes, yes, she knew.

Kaine had come for her as everyone predicted. Yet, she'd stopped him dead in his tracks with the only thing that could. Confessions of love that didn't exist love for Luka. That stopped him cold.

He finally heard the word no.

There wasn't time to mourn for Kaine. She was leaving London. Holly asked for the security box to collect her personals and passport. The door attendant took her luggage and gift out to the car where Luka approached her, sweeping her up into his arms.

"Reach into my pocket. My card. All my numbers are on it, London, Paris, and L.A. You have my private mobile number if you have any problems between here and Gatwick. I'm flying on the Super Star, the *Hurrikaine* tour jet. I will be in Paris for three days and the hotel number is on the card. Don't hesitate to call if you need me. I'll arrive in L.A., on day four. Keep that night open we'll have our first date with a sunset." He paused. "I don't want to create any problems in your life. I want to add to your life. I will make you happy," he promised.

Holly wanted to tell him not to count on her. She needed to go home and to heal. That would take a long time, maybe forever. As she looked at him, he lit up, how had the sun known this was the perfect moment to shine glorious rays of sunlight about Luka's golden hair? To light him up like an angel?

Luka crooked his head and moved in kissing her so lovingly.

She moved closer to deepen the kiss, to drink in the addictive taste of him, hoping to leave him with a memory of her, hoping he'd forgive her for leaving him — abandoning him.

Luka Hunter hugged her like a man totally in love with her, turned and stepped into a Hackney Cab, never looked back and vanished. Someone, somewhere, needed him more than her.

That was fine.

Her golden angel rode out of her life.

Chapter Twenty-Three

SLIPPING AWAY

The street was cold without Luka. Holly wiped an escaping tear from her eye. She was no good at goodbyes, but it was best for all concerned.

Howard stood next to the sleek, white Bentley — her coach. A bodyguard sat on the passenger side of the front seat. Luka was not taking any chances that much had not changed. The press was not on duty. Was it too early in the morning? Or, was she already old news simply because she was no longer the Heart of the *Hurrikaine*? It didn't matter that she was unbearably alone again.

Holly passed cities full of people she would never know, but because of the headlines of the London papers, they had been privy to her dazzling fairy tale romance with Kaine. She pushed her doubts away, but a thick veil of mist blinded her because she was taken farther and farther away from the eye of the *Hurrikaine*. She was headed closer to her future at home in L.A.

Tears dropped, and she silently brushed them away.

Gatwick was bustling. She ducked into the bathroom, finished the last vial, and flushed the empty bottle. How much she had changed since she'd landed in London a lifetime ago.

As she walked out of the bathroom, she heard.

"Holly? Holly," with a familiar Parisian accent.

She turned to see Solange approaching.

"Holly, I'm so glad to see you before you left."

"Solange? What are you doing here?"

"It seems everyone's leaving this morning. I have to meet Ian's parents in California to start arrangements for our wedding. It will be a media event. Ian's off for Paris."

Solange looked at Holly sympathetically and then acknowledged her ensemble.

"This looks encouraging, you're wearing a *Hurrikaine* sweatshirt like me," and she smiled, "come here you need a hug."

Holly nodded her head in agreement. "Yes, I do need a hug."

Solange held her for a quiet moment and then scolded.

"Why didn't you call me back? Kaine damned near drove me mad, wanting me to intercede for him. He kept calling. *Talk to her yet?* And every time I had to say no and he sank deeper into his dark depression. I wanted to help patch things up between you."

"There is nothing to patch up," Holly snapped defiantly.

There was still no way for her to face Kaine without the crushing humiliation of her betrayal.

Holly changed the subject. "Headed for L.A.?"

They compared seat numbers.

"Let's see if we can sit together?" Solange suggested.

They walked down a spiraling staircase to another section of the airport. Out in the distance, Holly spotted the imposing black tour jet. A purple *Hurrikaine* logo splattered across the nose cone said the words — Super Star.

She started to turn away.

"No Holly, it's not that easy to walk away. You need to see," Solange challenged firmly.

Holly watched on as the band filed by one-by-one, heading toward the plane.

"I hope we're not too late," Solange added with haste.

Then Ian walked into view.

"My cheri," Solange chirped happily.

Ian turned and looked up at them high in the airport wing, separated by a thick, impenetrable glass. Ian's face lit up when he spotted Solange and vigorously waved to her.

"I've always said goodbye and waved from here when I can't travel with Ian."

Holly watched the newly engaged lovers send kisses of love air express to each other. Then Ian spotted her and vigorously waved to her. Holly waved back, but she didn't have the vigor of Ian.

Holly was terrible with goodbyes.

Then out of the edge of the foggy shadows walked a nightmare. A tall, dark, lonely figure — dressed as if in mourning. His dark hair flowed freely about his slumped shoulders. His head was hanging low as if in anguish heading for the gallows.

Kaine — she understood his pain.

A condemned man — cast adrift. An outlaw, no longer loved.

Kaine — looked broken-hearted, alone, and abandoned.

Holly couldn't allow herself the luxury to feel anything. If she did, her heart would splinter like a light cast onto a prism. And she couldn't tolerate having her heart shattered again.

"Look Holly! That's Kaine! He's so fucked up over what happened between you. That man down there loves you like no other woman in his life. Is there ice in your veins? What are you made of Holly? How can you stand here and let Kaine go?"

Holly threw back her head each breath strangling her. She clutched her heart filling with sharp stabbing pains. If Solange didn't stop her badgering soon, she'd be forced to the floor.

"I can't do this Solange," she complained fighting back her tears. She understood Solange's words were designed to blow her into reality, but how could Holly let Solange know, she didn't need to say anymore. It was all she could do to keep from pounding on the glass to stop him.

To reach out — to Kaine.

"Kaine's exasperatingly stubborn and exceedingly prideful man. Impossible for him to say he's sorry." Solange defended.

Holly glanced at her friend. Solange's soft brown eyes filled with unasked questions.

"But he has...." Holly testified whirling around to Solange.

Barely able to speak, her sobs so loud, Holly told Solange about the single rose, the room full of roses, the suitcase with his love notes, his song, and Slick.

"This was waiting for me at the hotel's front desk when I checked out."

She didn't have the heart to tell Solange, Kaine had come for her and he'd found her in Luka's arms again confessing her love.

She showed her the unopened box in her LV KeepAll.

Solange tore the lid off and pulled out an exquisite, white dressing gown with an Asset label. The enclosed card read.

Please, wear this in Paris ...
Tonight is our wedding night.
Don't let me leave without you.
I'll love you always, your <u>only</u> forever man.

"Kaine wants to marry you?" Solange's mouth dropped her eyes flew open.

"He proposed to me backstage at Friar Manor before everything turned ugly."

Solange's eyes expressed it all.

"Well, what the hell are you waiting for, Holly? He wants you to be his wife and wearing this by nightfall. Come on Holly, you have a private jet to catch. HURRY!" Solange screamed.

Holly snapped quickly. She watched him walking on the runway. She did want Kaine. She'd promised him forever and always. It was a case of relaying the urgent message to her feet.

"Okay." She blurted on impulse. "Let's go."

Solange grabbed Holly's hand and led her, weaving around passengers and airport staff, searching for the stairs that led down to the ground level. Down the stairs, they sprinted beyond the doors out into the freezing cold air and onto the slick tarmac.

Holly let go of Solange, dropped her luggage and Slick and passed her, expecting all her days of running to pay off, and forced herself with all the speed she could find in her pain-ravaged body, hoping she would catch the jet before the hatch door closed. She'd promised never to leave Kaine alone.

Holly pushed herself harder, harder. The pictures formed in

her mind, showing her everything that had happened to her. The last seven days of her life flashed through her mind as if thumbing through a scrapbook. All the love — so much love.

Kaine's smile, his dimples and the way he'd loved her for hours and days, and oh those nights. His eyes that told her he'd always love her. She remembered sitting in the studio playing music together, stealing kisses and riding the motorcycle freely with the wind in their faces and then hiding from the fans in the English countryside.

How elegant Kaine appeared standing beside the fireplace in the Castle — his home. She remembered, her magnificent Kaine, she remembered all the moments of joy, all the promises, and foreverness of their love. Her hand touched her earlobe where the mammoth-diamond stud and pulled on it gently. He'd loved her with his open heart.

Then, unexpectedly, she saw Sarah, up ahead.

Sarah.

In a flash, she remembered.

Everything.

Sarah's threats in the shadows of the corridor.

Next time you get in the way of Kaine, and me, I'll use this gun and you can count on all the chambers loaded. I will kill you with Kaine's gun. Next time you won't see me coming and I won't leave you alive. The way, Kaine, and Luka have been at each other's throats over you, guess who will spend the rest of his miserable life in jail for your murder.

Holly recalled the pressure of the cold barrel of the gun next to her head. She slowed her pace.

Sarah made it clear if she came around again the next time she'd leave her dead. And with Kaine and his blackouts.

Holly understood what Sarah's threat meant — Kaine would be charged with her murder.

How the hell had this happened?

She looked at Sarah, who reminded her of all that was malicious and deadly in rock 'n' roll. And how absurd it was that Luka and Kaine had worn weapons to protect themselves from death threats they'd perceived to come from outside the organization. But the deadliest threat came from within, from one of their own.

Luka, she pictured him in her mind, her beautiful angel, and his words so clearly.

Don't let Kaine or me, or anyone else make up your mind. You're strong you can do this.

Sarah cupped the elbow of a crushed and broken Kaine, guiding him up each step of the ramp stairs to the jet.

Holly stopped in her tracks.

Solange caught up with her.

"Why are you stopping?" she demanded, pulling Holly along the wet, slippery tarmac toward the jet, yelling at the top of her lungs.

"Come on, Holly. You're going to miss the damn jet. Kaine will go to Paris alone."

Solange's words carried her back to Kaine's note, begging her.

Please don't leave me alone.
Your only forever man.

But Holly's vision narrowed to Sarah.

She knew then she needed to protect the one and only man, she truly loved.

In those seconds, she realized she was strong and the second time she would let Kaine go.

Holly screamed at Solange, the tears welling in her eyes.

"He's not alone. Kaine has Sarah!"

They screamed at each other over the earsplitting sounds of the jet's high-pitched whine, and the engine's wind gusts strong enough to blow them into a foreign country.

"Holly, I can't stand here and argue, that jet is about to take off without you. Kaine loves you! You're the Heart of the *Hurrikaine*. You will never find a man like him to love you as he does. Holly catch that jet. NOW!"

"It's too late for Kaine and me," Holly muttered as hot stinging tears bit behind her eyes. Torment shattered her aching body, blending with an agony that exhausted her soul. It was the anguish and pain of having her heart ripped out of her chest.

Kaine disappeared with Sarah into the biting cold of the morning mist. Then the Super Star leisurely taxied down the runway as if to give her another chance to change her mind. She gathered all her strength and resolve, knowing her decision would keep Kaine safe. She watched the Super Star turn and taxi toward her.

Her grief-stricken tears flowed freely.

Her heart shattered to smithereens.

Holly raised her chin, listening to the deafening sound of the

Super Star's engines soar over her head. She watched Kaine's jet rise to kiss the hem of the gray London sky. All the while, her heart continued splintering into millions of pieces. Her grief so devastating that it shoved her to her knees, forcing her to let go.

The torture became unbearable.

She screamed aloud as if Kaine could hear her over the roar of the engines.

"Goodbye, my Precious One."

Chapter Twenty-Four

TIME WAITS FOR NO ONE

Holly collapsed on the tarmac believing she was trapped in a grotesque nightmare and she couldn't wake up. She sobbed because Kaine took her forever love with him.

Her body moved … gently. An arm lifted up to her knees.

She heard familiar voices.

"Holly?"

They were a blend of Solange's Parisian and another elegant British accent. She looked up confused, to find her golden angel.

"Everything will be all right, Babe."

Solange yelled angrily at Luka. "Why aren't you on the Super Star? Luka, what the hell happened to you?"

Holly pulled away to see what Solange meant. Luka's beautiful face bruised. His left eye practically swollen shut, his lip split and bleeding, his hand wrapped with a bandage, and blood was splattered down the front of his blue denim shirt.

"Luka?" Was all she managed.

"I fucking quit!" He blasted back, angry with Solange.

"That bastard said I was sacked! He can't sack me! I practically own his ass. I'm tired of taking his fucking abuse. And when he hit me, well, I couldn't hold back," he hollered.

"You — hit Kaine!" Solange yelled, demanding to know.

Holly glanced down at his hands. The knuckles of his right hand were bloody.

"He had it coming, and then more," he snapped.

"Oh Luka, how could you?" Solange remarked thoroughly disgusted. "You know how vulnerable Kaine is now!"

"Rubbish! Do I look like he is? He's a jolly big lad. Bollocks! He's not my problem anymore. Don't you have a plane to catch Solange?" Luka added pointedly.

"Yes, I suppose I do. Holly, we should go." Solange suggested.

"Holly stays with me. I don't plan to be without her any longer. I've ordered the CMT jet. She flies with me," Luka stipulated adamantly.

"You can't bully me, Luka. Let's go, Holly," Solange demanded, gently taking hold of Holly's forearm trying to free her from Luka's embrace.

Holly stood fast, sobbing, too filled with pain to string thoughts together. The tragic scene was too unbelievable. She'd sent Kaine away to protect his future.

She looked up into Luka's eyes and pleaded. "Can't Solange fly back with us?"

Luka shot a piercing look to Solange.

"It is better if we traveled separately." Luka firmly advised.

"He's right Holly. I'm a remind of the band. If you're going with him, you'll need a fresh start to put London behind you."

Solange looked up to Luka. She wasn't smiling. Clearly, she was loyal to Kaine. But what she did say surprised Holly.

"Take good care of her, Luka?"

"You know I will, Solange."

"Yes, I do and hope this works out the way you want. I suppose, for now, the best man won."

"It wasn't a competition Solange." Luka defended.

"Wasn't it Luka? Isn't it always? Never mind. It doesn't matter anymore."

"But it does," Luka argued.

"Holly needs to believe London wasn't a game. What's happened is not about the past, but about new feelings and building a stable future."

His words were ignored.

Solange already turned to Holly, gave her a sisterly hug, and then affirmed. "I'll call you when I set a wedding date. You promised to come and Ian expects you, Luka."

Holly noticed Solange forcing a smile. There was no perfect answer, any ending would have hurt someone, and, this time, and it was Kaine.

Luka gave Solange a quick, affectionate hug and promised. "I will see you become Mrs. Ian Montgomery. Thank you for letting me handle this my way."

Solange looked to Holly, forced a smile as she reached out to squeeze her hand and encouraged. "Be happy." Solange Beauvais turned and walked toward the airport terminal, gradually swallowed by a blanket of rolling fog.

Holly didn't have a chance to react. Luka slid his arm around her waist and guided her to a private area. A white Lear jet with the CMT logo awaited Luka's instructions.

Out of the hazy fog, a swarm of reporters stormed them before they could get up the ramp steps and safely into the jet. The minicams and camera lights flashed. She was amazed how quickly she become news again.

The Heart of the *Hurrikaine* catching a jet without Kaine and everyone wanted to know why.

Holly covered her tear-stained face as Luka hid her head under his leather jacket. The vultures of the press swarmed over them trying to snap a photo of the two of them.

Luckily, the questions were directed to Luka.

Why were Luka and Holly taking a different jet? But more importantly why together? Everyone clamored to know why Kaine and Holly were not flying together.

Should she answer them? Tell them their love affair was finished.

Luka protected her, single-handedly fighting the press all the way to the boarding ramp where they climbed the stairs and finally escaped into the CMT jet.

Inside was spacious and comfortable, complete luxury with three attendants. She wasn't worried that they were the only passengers. After hours of watching Luka sort and attend to papers and files, she'd settled down to think. She'd decided to tell Luka about Sarah, the gun, and her threats, soon, but not today.

She lost herself in short conversations with him.

Turbulence during the flight played havoc with Holly's tender rib cage and insomnia plagued her. Holly leaned into Luka's embrace. They didn't need to speak. They shared an unshakable bond. They'd endured the devastating landfall of the *Hurrikaine*, the worst part of the storm and thankfully, they both survived. The discoloration around both their eyes would force them to hide behind their Ray Ban sunglasses when they landed. However, it was L.A., who would know, who would care?

With the pilgrimage to the eye of the *Hurrikaine* over, the sleek, black limousine drove, them undetected through the familiar streets of Hollywood. She was taking Luka home to her place high in the canyon.

Luka spoke from the shadows. "Do you want a hit from the vial to take away the pain?"

"No, Luka. All the vials have brought me are heartache and destruction. Doesn't the cocaine ever get to you?"

"Babe," he admitted as if astonished by her observation.

"I'm sorry. I thought you knew. I never touch the evil powder. It's poison. I've been clean and sober for years. I learned to change the things I could, and that was me. Then again, I'm not a preacher. I figure, to each their own."

She was dumbfounded, but it was true. She'd never seen Luka indulge in cocaine. She'd been so high she'd assumed he was doing the lines along with her. She looked at him.

He raised his eyebrows. "Forgive me?"

"For what? In fact, I'm glad, Luka. I don't want to see another vial."

Luka put his arm around her. "As you wish Babe, and I'm glad to hear you say that."

And he kissed away any thoughts of sex, drugs and rock 'n' roll, or Kaine Walker, as only Luka could.

Chapter Twenty-Five

YOU GOT IT

West Hollywood, California

Day 8

Holly wasn't ready. The barrage of media that circled her house acted like a hungry posse. Luka pushed and shoved his way to her front door, but without bodyguards, he was one man against an army.

From nowhere Holly spotted help on the way.

"Brett. Over here, help us get to my door."

Brett pushed his way to Holly, dressed in his typical, elegant, tailored suit. A warmhearted smile grew on her face so glad to see him. He grabbed her arm in a vice grip and she flashed back to the ugly encounter with Kaine down in Hell at the manor.

"Why didn't you answer any of my messages?" He demanded to know with a *nasty* expression pasted on his handsome face.

Holly started to speak, but he answered his own question.

"Too busy fucking the rock star?"

Her eyebrows flew up, hcr mouth dropped open. Cameras whirled, and the reporters flung tape recorders in her face.

"Not now Brett." She pleaded and turned to step into her cottage.

"Then when? After the next rock band comes to town?"

Luka stepped between them. He looked Brett squarely in the eyes. Luka challenged him with a tone, thick with a warning. "You owe the lady an apology."

"Who are you? The rock star that's fucking her? The Heart of the *Hurrikaine* ... Holly, how could you? Jon would be ashamed of you."

Brett's piercing words seriously wounded her. Holly slumped onto Luka's body. She'd thought of all people, Brett would understand. He would be happy she'd found someone to love? But no? And standing in the middle of an assault by the media wasn't the time to find out why.

"That's enough. Bloody leave her alone. And get the fuck out of here," Luka demanded shoving Brett in the chest with his hands.

"I'll leave when I'm damn well ready. Who are you anyway? Her rock star lover?"

"That's none of your fucking business." Luka pointed out with his teeth clenched.

"Holly, is my fiancée, and that does make it my business!"

"The way I hear it, the lady has no plans to set a date."

Brett's face acknowledged Luka's truth and raged with anger. The cameras flashed and video cameras whirled. The reporters were elated to have this melodrama unfolding before them.

Brett pulled Holly closer and growled in her ear. "This stunt of yours cost me the election. No D.A. has a wife out fucking rock stars. Any hopes and dreams of me in political office went when you fucked that long haired asshole. How fucking could you?" Brett's selfish attack shocked Holly to her core.

So, it was about what was right for Brett? Never her. How stupid could she have been? But things weren't getting any easier. She couldn't find her house key. Luka was seething and so was Brett. The press loved it. Holly wanted to tell Luka to smash the glass and climb inside through her window. But it was too late.

Brett shoved Luka. "Step aside. I have more to say to her."

Holly never saw Brett so angry with her.

"You've said all your bloody well going to say to her," Luka stated flatly.

Brett pushed Luka and tried to take a swing at him, missing. Luka threw down his Ray Ban sunglasses and retaliated. Luka did not miss and Brett took the full brunt of Luka's pent up anger at Kaine.

The reporters didn't know whether to set down their equipment and stop the fight or root Luka on to victory. Brett was clearly no match for Luka's fury.

As Holly found the house key and opened the door to dart in, Luka connected with Brett's jaw again and knocked him inside the cottage. Luka followed slamming the door shut with his foot.

Holly quickly locked the door.

Brett lay flat out on her carpet. Blood gushed from his nose and trickled from the corner of his mouth and then down his chin, ruining his crisp, white polo shirt.

"You're going to be fucking sorry, Holly. I'm going to sue this bastard for assault and battery and take every penny he has."

"Brett, calm down. Can you hear yourself?" Holly admonished shocked beyond belief.

Brett caught his breath and wiped his mouth. The sight of his own blood enraged him again.

Luka braced himself ready for another round with Brett.

"Holly, call your dog off me. Let me talk to you for one damn minute." He pleaded reigning in his anger.

"Don't Holly," Luka warned none too happy to be called a dog. "You don't have to listen to anything this tosser has to say."

"It's okay, Luka. Please. I'll take him outside on the patio."

"No, every reporter in town will hear you. I'll go. I have a few phone calls to make."

"Luka?" She looked into his storming blue eyes. Intense eyes that warned, Brett Templeton, had one chance, one.

"I'm bloody well all right." Luka turned to Brett and pointed his finger in his face. "You hurt her or upset her and you'll be picking up the pieces of your face."

"Okay, okay." Brett pleaded, holding his hands up in a pose of surrender. Brett's facial expression said he suddenly realized Luka not only outweighed him but also had a taste for his blood.

"Holly?" Brett squeaked out.

Luka backed down reluctantly. He kissed Holly squarely on the mouth to confirm how things were. He slowly walked to where Holly showed him the doorway to a small, intimate garden. Holly hustled up a towel and produced ice cubes for Brett's swelling face and another for Luka's hand.

Brett looked away from her taking the wrapped ice and placing it on his chin. His facial expression was scrunched as he winced in pain. "I counted on you, Holly. But I see that things have changed. You've moved on with your life."

"What are you talking about, Brett?"

"I've always loved you since we took the blood oath to protect each other. I realize now, you have honored that oath all these years by staying loyal and faithful to me. Something I took for granted. But we both know we aren't IN love with each other. And what I said about Jon earlier. Well, he'd be so proud of you finding your own life. I wish he could say the same about me."

Brett hung his head sheepishly. "Where do we go from here?"

"What are your thoughts?"

"Winning the Collin's murder trial put me, us, on the map. But I resigned from the firm this morning because of the headlines of your trip to England and the rock star. That caused problems, and well, it has all the partners angry. Your job will be hell without me there."

"So I'm unemployed too?"

"I guess so. I'm considering opening an office back east if you're interested. I'm surprised to say I'm okay, except for how awful I've treated you for all these years. Everything I did, I thought it was the best for you, you do know that?"

Brett stepped closer and insisted. "I do want you to be happy and if this rock star can do it. Well?"

"Luka's not a rock star. I wasn't strong enough to handle his lifestyle. But Luka, he's an incredible man."

"He has a great right arm," Brett announced and smiled to break the biting tension. "It would appear he loves you a lot."

"I believe he does."

"And you love him?"

"I care for him," and what she didn't say was that she let the love of her life go, as her hand found its way to the diamond stud.

"Then with your permission, I withdraw my proposal of marriage."

Holly opened a drawer and pulled the five-carat diamond from the corner. "I wouldn't have made you a good wife."

"Yes, you would have. You've proven that. It's, I wouldn't have made you a good husband. I love you, Holly. I always will. You're the closest family I have. I hope one day you'll find it in your heart to forgive me."

"I love you too Brett, all is forgiven."

Brett Templeton walked over and Holly handed him the ring and then stood up to hug him. He graciously kissed her on the cheek as Luka walked in giving Brett, a careful eye.

"The lady says you love her. If you don't take care of her, you will have to answer to me." Brett vowed, rubbing his swelling jaw and then applied the bag of ice.

Luka spread a forced half-smile.

Brett took a step closer to Luka, reached out to offer his hand. "I'm sorry we got off on the wrong foot or should I say fist?"

The moment's levity was welcomed and Luka wearily accepted Brett's apology.

Brett hugged Holly again, turned and walked out the door to be engulfed by the media.

Luka sank into a nearby chair. "Fuck Holly, what a bizarre homecoming! What was all that?"

"That was the answer to an important question."

Holly went into her kitchen and took a few moments to collect her thoughts while brewing Orange Pekoe tea. Then poured two steamy mugs. She took Luka by the hand and led him to her bed.

"I like this part of the homecoming," Luka teased smiling mischievously.

"Lie down and relax while I tell you Brett's news."

Holly lay in Luka's arms. It had been a full morning, and all was quiet outside her cottage.

Luka broke the silence first. "The engagement is off and you have lost your job as well?"

"I have some savings. After a long rest, I'll find another one." She assured and looked up at her sweet angel. How much had changed in seven days?

Luka gently pulled her up onto his chest into his warm embrace and kissed her to oblivion.

She lay there thinking about how she and Kaine had set the world ablaze. However, he was the forbidden fruit, a rock star. He was meant to dream of, but never to have. He belonged to the entire world.

She'd found her answer.

No, she couldn't love two men at the same time. She could only love one. With that admission, she smiled and tugged on her ear.

Holly lay with her beautiful Luka, her sexy Luka, steady,

dependable and so madly in love with her. How had she the good fortune to land on her feet?

Luka kissed her with his unrestrained passion as only Luka could until she exploded with lusty desire. When Luka let go of her, she knew she had made the right decision, at last, to leave in her past, Jon De La Guerra, Brett Templeton and now Kaine Walker. Luka Hunter might be her future.

By mid-afternoon, Holly had cleaned up and changed into a baggy white T-shirt, comfortable, light blue Levi's and royal blue canvas shoes. She'd finished French braiding her hair when Luka came close. He smelled so delicious after his shower. His eye was open and the ice packs forced the swelling to recede. He'd had his luggage delivered with hers and changed into a crisp blue and white pinstripe, straight-collared shirt, and dark blue 501 button-up Levi's and Nautica boots.

"I've had my car delivered. I believe we have a date for dinner."

"Great, I'm starving. How will we get past the reporters?"

"Let's say I've called in a favor. We should have muscle intervene soon."

She laughed, "Do you know people everywhere?"

He smiled light-heartily, cocked his head to the side boyishly. "I guess I do."

Luka opened the door and sure enough, they walked without pause to his new, black convertible, Corvette. She was impressed with his power to persuade the press to back off as well as his choice of car.

"I see they are bloody well able to be reasoned with," Luka chortled.

He drove down Sunset Blvd., caught the 405 to the 101

freeway, and headed north. He drove for a long while, the majority of the time he was on the phone contacting everyone in the music industry, or so it seemed to Holly.

"Where are we headed?" she asked between calls.

"I thought you could show me around, Santa Barbara?"

Holly smiled warmly, placing her hand over his. Luka had taken to heart her tragic story of how hard it was to go home. Holly called her family and her mother's joy-filled voice said she would set the table with her finest linens and tableware because Holly was bringing home a man.

They drove through the quaint seaside community. At one exit, Holly asked Luka to pull off the freeway. It led to the cemetery.

"I've never been here because I've never summoned the courage to say goodbye to Jon," she confessed.

"Let's go together, Babe. We'll say goodbye to Jon." Luka offered, holding her hand, giving her the necessary strength.

Holly stood by the grave, free at last. She knew Jon would have liked Luka.

Luka wove his fingers into hers and tightly squeezed.

And for a moment a peace filled her, she was positive she'd felt Jon's blessing.

They left and continued up the coast until she gave Luka more directions and then to pull off to a narrow road. She took him to a tiny private beach near her parent's house. They strolled along the water's edge. She watched the brilliant California sun with Luka. It was the largest globe, she'd ever seen. The orange ball dropped low in the sky, finally at rest.

Luka and Holly hadn't walked a moment when his cellular rang.

He stopped, shrugged his shoulders, and threw her a plea for forgiveness look. His eyebrows arched as he pulled it out.

But she intercepted the phone and flung it far into the white-capped waves.

He smiled. And when Luka smiled, he lit up the whole world.

Holly turned and took Luka's hand.

His eyes sparkled as only they could when he looked at her.

She reminded him. "Our first sunset."

Luka stopped and took her in his arms. Luka with his fucking blue eyes-to-die-for, his long golden pirate hair, doing what he did best, kissing her breath away.

When he let go of her, he whispered in her ear. "I can make you happy."

She smiled and whispered in his ear. "You already have, Angel Eyes."

Luka kissed her, taking her to their private place.

What the hell was she going to do about Luka when the sun went down tonight?

She coiled her arms around his neck, pushed her hips into him, and wrapped her leg around his.

She had a plan....

TO BE CONTINUED...

Dear Reader,

Ready to purchase **BLOOD**, part 1, in the Hollywood series? Please take a moment and leave a few comments about your favorite scenes wherever you purchased **BETRAYAL**. It is crucial to the series to have immediate feedback while the pleasure from the story is fresh in your mind. Thank you for your valuable support. YOU ROCK!

The rock 'n' roll fairy tale has ended...

A distraught Holly Hill is home in Hollywood, California. She has a secret, is emotionally devastated and heading dangerously close to drowning in a dark depression.

The knight on the white horse...

CMT executive, Luka Hunter, has Holly all to himself. Can he convince her she has the necessary strength needed for her healing and transformation?

Or... is he too late?

Will the vivid memories and dreams of Kaine Walker and their forever love continue to haunt her? Or will the secret that holds Holly captive drive her to destruction?

What will she do...
when her secret is out?

http://www.kewtownsend.com/

KEW TOWNSEND

Affairs of the Heart Series ~ London

HEART (Part 1), *TEMPTATION* (Part 2)
PROMISES (Part 3), *DEVOTED* (Part 4), *BETRAYAL* (Part 5)

Forthcoming:

Affairs of the Heart ~ Hollywood

BLOOD (Part 1), *SURRENDER* (Part 2),
LIASION (Part 3), *DECEPTION* (Part 4)

Ms. Townsend is a widow with a wonderful daughter, educator of school-age students, travel and movie buff, and writes romantic music fiction set in the 1960s-1980s rock scene in the *Affairs of the Heart Series*. She lives in sunny Southern California and loves to read under a palm tree with wave's crashing along the shoreline.

KEW's love of rock music began at a young age when she returned glass Coke bottles for change to buy 45 rpm records. Her interested moved from the music to the musicians, and living in Hollywood, interviewed the Beatles when they landed at Los Angeles International Airport. Acquiring a taste for the funny Englishmen, she began dating one of the Rolling Stones that exposed her to sex, drugs, and rock and roll. Later her memories surfaced in the *Affairs of the Heart Series* where she weaves her behind the scenes anecdotes with her long love of castles, mysteries, lightning, and thunder into a romantic suspense story. Her master's degree in Cultural Anthropology and Archaeology adds to her world travels, and flavor to her novels.

CONTACT KEW
kewtownsend.com

Leave a message, a review, and sign up for NEWSLETTER. Be first to hear about new releases, preorders, sales, prizes, giveaways, and fun events.